W9-BBA-936

The Big Drive

**Center Point
Large Print**

**This Large Print Book carries the
Seal of Approval of N.A.V.H.**

The Big Drive

WILL COOK

CENTER POINT LARGE PRINT
THORNDIKE, MAINE

This Center Point Large Print edition is published
in the year 2012 by arrangement with
Golden West Literary Agency.

The text of this Large Print edition is unabridged.
In other aspects, this book may
vary from the original edition.
Printed in the United States of America
on permanent paper.
Set in 16-point Times New Roman type.

ISBN: 978-1-61173-437-9

Library of Congress Cataloging-in-Publication Data

Cook, Will.
  The big drive / Will Cook. — Large print ed.
  p. cm. — (Center Point large print edition)
  Originally published under the pseudonym of Wade Everett.
  ISBN 978-1-61173-437-9 (lib. bdg. : alk. paper)
  1. Large type books. I. Title.
  PS3553.O5547B54 2012
  813´.54—dc23
                                                    2012004303

1

Colonel Mitchell Shannon didn't like his new command, and he didn't like dropping from brevet general, two stars, to light colonel, but the war was over and the south was in turmoil and the Union army was breaking up and he supposed he was lucky to revert to permanent rank and draw a military governorship, even if it was Texas.

A company of engineers built the post for him, and had trouble doing it for the Texans were an unruly lot and took to military control like cats take to water. But he had his assignment, and his command; two troops of cavalry, four companies of infantry, and supporting units, quartermaster and medical staff, and more trouble than any commander ought to have.

His post was Fort Stockton, an old post that had been renovated and enlarged to hold so large a command. To the south he had the Mexicans, who had never forgiven the Texans. In the north he had Indians who were itching for a big fight. Around him there were Texans, smarting because Lee surrendered and eager to have another go at it. And added to that, a confused government in Washington who established Negro police, billeted in the town of Marfa, not far to the southeast.

Prudence told him that it was better to leave his wife in the east; Texas would be a bit primitive for her, and she had endured her share of frontier service when she was younger. Shannon was fifty and she was only a few years younger and he wanted a tranquil life for her, not this heat and dust and danger. His children were grown, the boy an attorney, and both girls married, one to a naval officer which still irritated Shannon at times.

He was a well-kept fifty, slender, tall, flat in the belly and stern in the eye. His once dark hair was nearly all gray now, but his eyebrows and thick mustache remained brown. Thirty years of service had given him a bit of a reputation and every man in his command knew that he ran a taut post and gave him no nonsense about it.

In the month and a half since his assumption of command, Shannon had been studying every report, every newspaper, sorting through each scrap of information and rumor that came his way, and when he was ready, he called his company commanders to headquarters, and told them to prepare the post for a general inspection. They were surprised, but offered no objection although the nearest general was in Ohio and had no intention of visiting this desolate outpost.

A day of fevered activity got the grounds in raked condition, the buildings freshly calcimined, and the stable area smelling reasonably fragrant. Then Shannon sent his aide off on a fast horse with his personal invitations, and sat back and waited.

The Texans came, all dressed in Confederate uniforms, and the post got its general, Nathan Pritchard, and his two sons, Major Nixon Pritchard, and Captain Owen Pritchard. There was a gaggle of colonels and some more majors, and Colonel Shannon presented them to his command in a full dress inspection, then took them on a tour of the post. Afterward they went to the officers' mess, which had been decorated for the occasion, including a large Confederate flag, and that, coupled with gallons of good whiskey, put them in a fair frame of mind.

"Gentlemen, I propose a toast," Shannon said, rising with his glass. "To the south, sirs, and that great leader, General Robert E. Lee."

They were willing to go along with that, and he wanted to get them into the notion of saying yes; a man could beat himself before he started by antagonizing them.

General Pritchard had something to say and stood up; instantly the room was hushed of talk and this confirmed Shannon's suspicions, that Pritchard was indeed the most powerful man in these parts. "I would like to say, sir," Pritchard said, "that this courtesy is most delightful and unexpected. It has been our opinion, sir, in view of the niggah police, that the yankee politicians mean to rub our faces in the dirt. However, I am glad to say that each of us feels honored by your acknowledgment of our military rank."

He sat down and there was applause. Shannon used the interval to gain control of his voice, then said quietly, "General, it was not my decision to appoint Negro police to the state of Texas. Had it been mine to make, they wouldn't be here. Theirs is a difficult, if not impossible, position. But they are here, commanded by reserve officers who never saw a southern soldier, and who are now trying to make up for it. This post has been established to preserve law and order, to promote commerce in Texas, and to help you put your money on a sound basis. You are all property owners and you have thousands of cattle and no place to sell them. You've been paying in script you've issued yourselves, but you know that can't go on forever. We've got to bust out, gentlemen. We've either got to bring money to Texas, or take the things Texas can produce where the money is."

A short, blocky man in gray stood up. "Colonel Daniels, sir. Race Daniels. I have friends in east Texas, sir, and according to them the land is being overrun by Yankee political opportunists. Land is being bought up left and right. They'll start moving here next. Do you know, sir, there's a law on the books in Travis county, prohibiting a Texan from carrying a pistol?"

"I had heard that such legislation was attempted," Shannon admitted.

"Without guns to protect ourselves," Daniels said, "we'll be at the mercy of every carpetbagger in the north."

"My orders, gentlemen, are clear. Help Texas rebuild herself," Shannon said. "And by golly, I intend to do that. If the situation grows so bad that you are denied the right to protect yourself, I'll issue arms and ammunition from my own arsenal."

The applause was ringing. He had to hold up his hands to quiet them. "Gentlemen, I have issued orders with all my officers that your name alone is sufficient to admit you to the post at any time. We fought a war on opposite sides. That was a tragedy, that we were so divided. But the war is over, and another is beginning, the war for the survival of Texas. It is a war we must win. To do that we must put aside old matters of disagreement and pull together. I believe I can rely on you gentlemen to lead Texas out of this trouble as you were once relied on to lead her sons in battle."

The meeting ended on a friendly tone and Shannon saw them all into their buggies and off the post, then he went to his office and found Lieutenant Malcolm, his aide, waiting. He helped Shannon out of his dress uniform and into a comfortable blouse.

"Very effective speech, sir," Malcolm said. "You have them eating out of your hand, so to speak."

"Yes," Shannon said, taking the offered light for his cigar. "It's better than having them snapping to take a bite out of me, isn't it? Send a message to Captain Dane at Marfa. Tell him I'd like to have a talk with him. He's got to keep those Negro police under control. Every time a Texas man sees one with a badge on his blue shirt, it's like throwing coal oil on a fire. I don't want an explosion in my district."

"Yes, sir. I'll have a dispatch rider off in twenty minutes."

"I'd be a fool if I thought these southern gentlemen really trust me," Shannon said. "Their policy is to wait and see what I do next. I want an order issued that all men on leave to towns will go without firearms or weapons of any kind. Fistfight trouble can always be smoothed over, but gunfight trouble can't."

Malcolm nodded and made notes. "Anything else, sir?"

"Yes, I want that dress ball to come off as planned this Saturday night," Shannon said. "The old south is dead and gone, but they remember and many of these Texas cattlemen are from the heart of Dixie. I want the regimental band to work on all the Stephen Foster songs they can remember." He puffed on the cigar. "They're like kids who can't bring themselves to put away their toys and go to bed; they come here dressed in their fancy uniforms as though they were still in the army." He waved his hand. "Get on with it, Mr. Malcolm."

"Yes, sir." He closed his notebook and stepped out and went into the adjutant's office. "Here's a couple of dispatches the old man wants sent. Pretty good show this afternoon, wasn't it?"

The adjutant smiled. "It's going to have to be more than that, Mr. Malcolm. You can only pretend so long, then it catches up with you."

"You're too glum," Malcolm said. "Hell, they lost the war. What do they really expect?"

"I guess to be left alone," Lieutenant Heinz said. He looked up, his blunt face wearing a trace of worry. "You know, I think the old man will get the job done, but they'll hate him for it. When I was a kid, I caught a skunk in the woods, not knowing any better. My father bathed me in coal oil and that smelled worse than the skunk."

"Not to everybody else, Carl."

"But to me, and I was the one who had the stink, remember."

"All in the point of view," Malcolm said, turning to the door.

"Exactly," Heinz said.

He wrote out the dispatches, sent an orderly with them to the sergeant major's office, then went to the stable for his horse. With his paperwork caught up, he felt that a ride would do him good, get him away from the oppressing efficiency of headquarters. He left the post and

11

rode east until he came to a cluster of ranch buildings, then took the rutted road and went on by. Two miles farther he came to the town, just one street with close-pressed board buildings set in the middle of rolling prairie.

There was some traffic on the street, a few horsemen and he circled a parked buggy in order to reach the hitchrail. His horse passed close to the team and caused one to throw its head and Heinz reached out quickly, grabbed the reins and quieted the animal.

Then from the corner of his eye he noticed the woman sitting in the buggy. She said, "Thank you. She's a bit coltish yet."

"Indeed," Heinz said, taking off his hat. The buggy top shaded her and a bonnet tied firmly shaded her face further, but he could see that she was young and rather pretty.

A pair of horsemen rode past and tied up; Heinz noticed that they wore gray pants but thought little of it for a lot of Texans wore parts of their uniforms. It seemed to be the thing to do, even when they were getting a little thin at the bottom and knees.

A man came out of the store and stepped into the buggy. He looked sour around the mouth, like a man will when he's been denied money, and when he picked up the reins, Heinz moved his horse out of the way and the man drove off. As the rig passed down the street, the girl looked out and back, and he smiled and dismounted.

The two men in gray pants were standing on the saloon porch, watching, and when he went to step between them, one said, "Havin' a little talk with the lady?"

"I beg your pardon?" Heinz said.

The man laughed. "Now that's very polite. You was talkin' to a real southern lady there, soldier. I hope you said the right things."

"I think so," Heinz said and went to step on.

But the other man reached out and took him by the arm. "Just so we make sure, suppose you tell us what was said. You see, that's Nix Pritchard's girl there and we wouldn't want her insulted or nothin', now would we?"

"She wasn't insulted," Heinz said.

They nodded solemnly. "But we've only got your word for that, haven't we?"

None of this talk had been loud, but somehow it had attracted men from inside the saloon; they crowded around the door and more men along the walk stopped to observe and listen.

"My word is sufficient," Heinz said. He moved his arm but the man retained his grip and Heinz suddenly jerked and tore it away.

"Now I was tryin' to be nice," the man said cooly.

"So was I," Heinz said, "but you wouldn't let me. Care for a drink?"

"You tryin' to buy us?" one asked.

It tripped Carl Heinz's patience and he said, "If I was, it wouldn't cost me a drink."

"All you Yankees like trouble." He looked at his friend. "Ain't that so, Ed?"

"It is a fact." He looked at Heinz. "Did you ever do any fightin' in the war?"

"Yes," Heinz said.

Ed laughed. "Now doggone, how come they didn't shoot you? Was you hidin' all the time?"

"I felt like it most of the time," Heinz said. He glanced past the edge of the group and saw a squad of mounted Negro police riding past the end of the street and he knew the crowd on the sidewalk was attracting them for they quickened into a trot and came on. He gave Ed a shove, meaning to push him inside the saloon but the man interpreted it as the commencement of the fight, and he swung at Heinz.

There was no stopping it then and the Negro police came on, riding right into the crowd. The sergeant was giving the orders and they used their clubs to make a path and two jumped down and grabbed the two Texans.

Heinz rushed to stop them but the sergeant blocked them off; he held Heinz back, showing his teeth and wide whites of the eyes. "You just stay heah, suh. We handle dis, suh."

They were handling it in a manner of speaking; the two Texans were bloody and handcuffed when the milling police parted enough for Carl Heinz to see.

"You all undah arrest," the sergeant said, "if you all don't clear out. Move on dere, I don't tell you again." He pushed and prodded with his club and the crowd broke up, but it was full of smoldering hate.

Ed looked at Heinz and grinned. "One of these days, soldier, these here niggers ain't gonna be around. Then we'll fix you up good."

Heinz felt like asking them who started it, and he felt like telling him that none of this was his doing, but he knew it wouldn't do any good.

The sergeant motioned with his club and the two Texans were taken off to jail. Heinz said, "Did you have to use the clubs, sergeant?"

"Suh, de white officer he say you don' fool around. You use de clubs. Dat's what ah do, just like he say."

"Yes," Heinz said. "Of course."

He turned to his horse and stepped into the saddle and rode out of town, wishing that he had never taken the notion to come in at all.

2

Lieutenant Heinz knew there was nothing he could do immediately for the two Texans, so he returned to the post. Captain Paul Dane had been summoned, and the matter could be taken up when he arrived, but this knowledge did not dispel the simmer of anger, or the sense of justice outraged by the whole affair. Of course, the two Texans had confronted him without provocation and made a fuss, but he could excuse that as being pride and foolishness. The action by Dane's police could not be dismissed in Heinz's mind so casually; clearly Captain Dane, faced with the complicated and explosive problem of dealing with naked hatred for his untrained Negro police, had instructed his men to hit first and let him sort out the answers later. Clearly too, this was not going to work.

As soon as he reached his office he went to work on some reports that had come in while he'd been gone, and he was working on these when Colonel Shannon opened his door.

"Ah, you're back, Heinz. Would you step in please?" He stood aside while Heinz walked in, then Shannon closed the door. "It's come to my attention that General Pritchard has two daughters. Heinz, I would like you to select two appropriate gifts for me to present to them when I go there to dine."

"I haven't the slightest idea—"

"You'll think of something," Shannon said. "Don't disappoint me now."

"Yes, sir," Heinz said and made a note of this. "Sir, while I was in town, two Texans were beaten by police and hustled off to jail. I would like to discuss this with Captain Dane when he arrives."

Shannon looked at him. "What is there to discuss?"

"Their release, sir. The matter was entirely between myself and the Texans."

"So you were mixed up in it," Shannon said. "Heinz, I expect my officers to be aloof from these local matters."

"This was a personal misunderstanding, sir, that did not warrant such harsh treatment by the police."

"I'm afraid we must let Dane decide that," Shannon said. "He has his authority."

"He's abusing it, sir."

The casualness left Shannon's expression. "Lieutenant, may I remind you that you are an officer in the United States Army, and your remark was directed at your superior. Surely you don't value your career so lightly—"

"I value the truth, sir, and feel that my comment was just."

Shannon stroked his chin. "You are teetering on the borderline of some difficulty, Mr. Heinz. I suggest you take some time and think this over."

"Respectfully, colonel, I've thought it over," Heinz said. "We both know, sir, that we are not being honest with these people. This policy of—"

"That's enough!" Shannon snapped, then softened his tone. "Carl, what's the matter with you?" He waved his hand. "I understand your idealism, but there's a time and a place for it, and this isn't it. In the past I've admired your adherence to principle, but we're carrying it too far. You've got to make the bargain now, with yourself, as we all have. Texas is whipped. We'll save what we can, hurt whom we must, and not cry about any of it."

"Sir, these two men who were thrown in jail, they understand none of this. All we've done is make two enemies. God knows how many more we'll make." He spread his hands. "Texas is infested with lawless men. Why are they that way, sir? Have they been driven to it?"

"Hogwash!" Shannon said flatly. "A man is good or he's bad. It's ridiculous to continue this conversation, Carl; it'll only make me mad and get you into trouble."

"Yes, sir. But I'd like to say one more thing."

"What is it?"

"A man can't go through life constantly adjusting the values by which he regulates himself. For some time now I've been aware that a disagreement exists between what I believe, and the policies I'm ordered to follow. These compromises, sir, are not easy to make. I don't feel that I can make any more of them. As a consequence, I'd like to submit my resignation from the service."

Colonel Shannon stared. "You can't mean that."

"I do, sir."

Shannon turned to his desk and sat down.

"Carl, this is a big step; look what you're throwing away."

"Yes, but I've asked myself if I wouldn't be throwing away more if I remained in the service."

"All right," Shannon said. "Submit your resignation. I'll forward it with my endorsement." He looked steadily at Heinz. "When did you want this to take effect?"

"Immediately, sir."

"Very well. Have the orderly send Mr. Malcolm in. I'll have you relieved before evening mess."

"Thank you, colonel."

"Heinz, what will you do? Go back east?"

"No, I'll stay here." He smiled. "My resignation doesn't mean I'm running out on the job. I'd like to work with less—restraint."

"I see," Shannon said. "Heinz, we both can't be right. If I'm wrong, I'll look a bit of the fool, won't I?"

"More than a bit, colonel. Will there be anything else?"

"No." He stood up and offered his hand. "Good luck, Carl. You'll be hard to replace."

Heinz stepped out and met Malcolm; the young man seemed always on the run, and Heinz waved him right on into the colonel's office without knocking, a breach of etiquette committed before he had a chance to think. Then Heinz heard the colonel roar and he went out, smiling, thinking: there's nothing like getting off to a good start.

19

He went to the sutler's store and bought some clothes, then went to his quarters to pack. Unlike these rebels, he couldn't go around wearing part of his uniform for he wanted nothing to keep reminding them that he was a Yankee.

They'd remember it easily enough.

His uniforms were sorted out and given to his striker to sell, not a difficult job for most of the officers had need of an extra blouse or pair of pants or boots. His pistol and holster he kept, along with shot pouch and cap box; the rest went by the board and by evening mess he had disposed of everything, said his goodbyes, and checked out with Lieutenant Malcolm, who was now adjutant and not liking it much. The job carried a lot of authority and a good deal more responsibility, but a man stood little chance of promotion there.

With the papers in his pocket, Heinz mounted up and cleared the post. It was not easy to give up this life for he had chosen it years before, adjusted himself to it, and had been satisfied with it—until recently. Military occupation did not bother him, even if it meant subjecting the Texans to an iron authority. But this wasn't the right kind of authority. Texas was a big, rich prize, and it was Heinz's opinion that she was being readied for the land-grabbers and the speculators, to pick her bones, and all in the name of authority. The army would be blamed for it afterward, and that galled him.

He returned to town at dark and went to the jail and found a fat Negro sergeant in charge. Heinz said, "You have two prisoners here. Has bail been set yet?"

"We got fifteen here, boss. Which two you all want?"

"The two who were arrested today on the main street."

"Oh, dem. Twenny dollah apiece, suh."

Heinz paid the fine and the sergeant signed the release and the receipt, then sent a jailer back for the two men. They came out, stared at Heinz, then one of them laughed.

"Well lookee there, Ed. He's still around!"

"Did you pay our fines, mister?" Ed asked.

"Yes," Heinz said. "You shouldn't have been taken to jail in the first place."

"Now I gotta agree to that," Ed said. "The name's Leslie. This is my cousin, Joe." Then he frowned. "You ain't got your soldier suit on."

"Our discussion this afternoon was interrupted," Heinz said pleasantly. He pointed to Ed Leslie. "I'll take you first if your cousin thinks he can stay out of it. Or does it take two of you Texans to whip a Yankee?"

"Why, I do believe that man means to fight us," Joe said, smiling. "You go ahead, and don't you hurt him too bad because I want to get in a lick or two before his eyes roll over."

"It wouldn't be too smart to mix it up in

21

here," Ed said. "Suppose we go out of town?"

"Suits me," Heinz said and stepped outside.

It took them a few minutes to get their horses, and they joined him and they put the buildings behind them and the Leslies stopped by a dark, rotting barn at the west edge of town.

Heinz took off his pistol belt and laid it on the ground, then put his coat on top of that, and his hat. Ed Leslie was dancing about, shuffling his feet as though he just couldn't wait to get at it and when Heinz motioned, Ed Leslie came on with a rush, meaning to tackle. Heinz let the man get to him, then he simply fell down, grabbed Leslie by the back of the belt, and heaved him up and over. Leslie struck hard and Joe said, "Ed, this ain't no time to get clumsy."

Leslie was getting up and he stood in a crouch for a moment, one hand wiping his face. Then his feet were pumping and he charged in, swinging a high kick when he thought the distance was about right. Heinz let the kick bump his thigh and it hurt him some, but he caught the foot, swung it high and plopped Ed Leslie flat on his back.

Joe was jumping up and down. "Damn it, stop that fancy stuff and get to lickin' him! You're goin' to wear yourself out gettin' up!"

A sour look was passed to Joe Leslie, then Ed knotted his fists and shuffled forward. He swung hard and wide and Heinz bounced it off his shoulder and caught Leslie flush on the jaw. The man's head snapped back and he fell again and dust rose and Joe's dancing became more excited.

"Let me at him! You ain't doin' nothin' but fallin' down!" Joe yelled.

"Hell, try it if you know it all," Ed Leslie said and sat there in the dust.

Joe didn't wait for Heinz to turn around, he bounded for him and jumped on his back and Heinz simply bent at the waist and threw Joe over his head. He struck hard, rolled, and sat up, his expression surprised.

"That damned ground's hard," he said and got to his feet.

Heinz started after him, then stopped. "Horsemen!" he said. "The police. Let's get out of here!" He scooped up his belongings and they mounted up and cut toward a row of trees fifty yards to the south. They barely reached this cover when the mounted police arrived. A few men had lanterns and they made a search of the yard and Heinz knew they saw the tracks but there was no attempt made to follow them. Finally, after some milling around, the squad went back to the center of town and Ed Leslie breathed a sigh of relief.

Heinz said, "You want to finish it here?"

The Leslies looked at each other, then Ed said, "Doggone it, he's the quarrelsomest cuss I ever run into. Did you ever see the beat of it, Joe?"

"I never did," Joe admitted. "I can see how come the war got started." Then he grinned. "I guess we're square now, Yankee. You go along with that?"

"Why not," Heinz said. "You fellas live around here?"

"Nope," Ed said. "We only come in to rob the bank."

Heinz sat in stunned silence for a moment, then said. "You what?"

"Oh, there warn't no money in it," Joe said. "We give up the idea and headed for the saloon. Ed's got a fifty cent piece."

"Where do you live?"

Joe waved his arm at the prairie. "Where we put down a blanket. We got a ranch about forty miles south of here, but there's no sense in workin' it. You can't give cattle away if they was rounded up."

Heinz thought about this for a moment, then said, "Suppose I go back to town and buy some grub. We might share a fire tonight and a pan of biscuits."

"That's a better idea than fightin'," Ed Leslie said. "We'll wait here 'cause we don't want nothin' more to do with the police. It's too damned easy to get on a wanted poster these days, and with money scarce, the bounty hunters will take you in for a ten dollar reward."

Heinz left them and rode back to town and when he passed the jail he noticed the horses tied in front and was relieved to see that they'd given up the search. He went into the general store and bought a side of bacon, four pounds of coffee, some flour and rice and beans, a skillet, a small pot, and something to eat out of.

While the clerk was adding the bill, a young officer walked in, looked around and then came over to Heinz. He came to attention and saluted. "Lieutenant, I thought you'd left town with those two men. I'm Lieutenant Baker, sir."

He doesn't know I'm out of the army, Heinz thought, and kept his mouth shut. "At ease, Mr. Baker. What's the trouble?"

"Well, I'm not sure there is any trouble now, sir. However, I'd like to enclose in my report why you paid the fine of those two men."

"They shouldn't have been arrested," Heinz said.

"But they were fighting."

"They were not fighting," Heinz said flatly. "*I* will testify to that, if I have to."

"I see. Yes, sir. Still I'll have to report this to Captain Dane. He judges each case on its individual merits, sir."

"Exactly what does that mean, Mr. Baker?"

"Captain Dane likes to review the record of each prisoner, sir, in case they are wanted outlaws."

"Wanted by whom?"

"The police, sir."

"I see," Heinz said, "and who sets the fines?"

"Captain Dane, sir."

Heinz paid the clerk and picked up his sack. "When you write your report, tell Captain Dane that I think his whole system stinks to high heaven."

Color drained from Baker's cheeks. "You can't mean that, sir."

"You may quote me," Heinz said and stepped to the door. But he stopped there and turned back. "Where is the throne of this almighty person?"

"His office is in Marfa, sir, but I wouldn't expose those sentiments, sir—" He closed his mouth because Heinz had gone on out and was riding out of town.

The clerk said dryly, "You fellas have a hard time gettin' anyone to pay any attention to you, don't you?" Then he went to the back of the store and left Baker standing there alone.

3

They camped in a grove of trees along a creek five miles from town and had a good meal and afterward stretched out on their blankets and looked at the brightest stars hung against the blackest of nights.

Joe Leslie belched and said, "I do say that was a good feed. Best I've had for a month. Ain't that so, Ed?"

"Pickin's is poor, for a fact," Ed admitted. "And

much as I hate to admit it, it's gonna get poorer." He turned his head and looked at Heinz. "You've got to lose a war to find that out."

"It all comes down to money," Heinz said. "There just isn't any. It doesn't matter how many cattle a man has, if he can't sell them he's worse off than if he had none." He raised himself on an elbow. "Do either of you know General Pritchard?"

They shook their heads. "How come you want to know?" Ed asked.

"Because I want to talk to him," Heinz said.

Joe laughed. "Well, you know his youngest, Nan."

"I do?"

"Hell, she was the filly in the buggy," Ed said. "Didn't you know?"

"No, I didn't know," Heinz said. "Can you take me to Pritchard?"

They looked at each other, then Ed nodded. "Tonight?"

"Yes."

He got up and began to roll his blankets while Joe stomped out the fire. They saddled up and ten minutes later were mounted and crossing the creek. Ed Leslie swung eastward and they rode for better than an hour before Heinz saw lights in the distance, and it was almost another half hour before they dismounted in the yard. Pritchard's house was huge, three storeys with wide porches

27

running all around and a front door big enough to drive a carriage through.

Two men came from the shadows of the yard with rifles, then they recognized the Leslie boys and relaxed. "Who's he?" one asked, nodding to Heinz.

"A friend of Miss Nan's," Ed Leslie said.

The man grunted and said, "Come on to the bunkhouse. Give you a drink anyway. Home-made, but it's got a kick."

They walked away before Heinz could stop them, and he stood there, looking after them, then at the big door and wondering what he should do.

A servant opened the door and came to the porch and he said, "Would you inform Miss Nan Pritchard that I've come to call?"

"Yes, suh. You all want to step inside the hall, suh?"

Heinz went in and stood there with his hat in hand while the servant went up a long, winding flight of stairs at the other end. The hallway would have stabled a company of mounts with ease. The ceiling was vaulted and a balcony ran all the way around it so that the second and third floors opened to this large entranceway.

A few minutes later he saw her coming down the stairs and as she walked toward him, a curious frown puckered her smooth forehead. Then she stopped in front of him and said, "You've presumed a great deal, sir. I don't believe

I know you, although there's something familiar about your face."

He smiled to ease his embarrassment. "We met in town, briefly. You were in the buggy and my horse frightened your horses and—"

"Of course, the officer. I didn't recognize you out of uniform." Then her frown reappeared. "That was a short acquaintanceship to warrant a social call—" She hesitated. "Why, I don't even know your name."

"Carl Heinz," he said quickly. "Please, let me explain. This is rude, I know, but I hope you'll forgive me. I asked the Leslie boys to bring me here because I wanted to talk to your father."

He could not be sure whether this amused her or made her angry. "My," she said, "that isn't very flattering, is it? I've known occasions when men have used my father to see me, but this is the first time anyone has gone the other way around."

"You're angry," he said. "I don't blame you. But I wish you'd listen to the facts before you judge."

"What are the facts?"

"I've resigned my commission," he said. "The reasons aren't important now, but it is important to discuss a matter with your father. I don't know him and doubt that he would see me just on my name alone. Believe me, I had no intention of leaning on our brief meeting but I was stranded at your door, and there was a servant waiting and—" He shrugged. "Oh, what's the use? I'm just getting myself in deeper."

She laughed and this surprised him. "Mr. Heinz, you haven't used any flattery on me. I think you're an honest man. Come along. Father's reading in the library."

She opened the door and went in first. Nathan Pritchard was in his easy chair by the fire, reading, and he looked around when she closed the door. Then he saw Carl Heinz and put the book aside.

"One of your new friends, Nan? I haven't met this gentleman."

"This is Carl Heinz, father."

"Recently of Colonel Shannon's staff, sir," Heinz said.

Pritchard didn't rear back, but his manner changed, becoming cooler. "A Yankee officer? What are you doing in mah house, suh?"

"General, I've resigned my commission. And I must talk to you. Certainly, sir, you can see no harm in hearing me out."

Pritchard thought a moment, then waved Heinz into a chair. He reached for the bell cord to get a servant, but Nan said, "Would you like a drink, father?"

"Perhaps Mr. Heinz—"

"Thank you, no," Heinz said. "General, I don't know where to begin. I suppose it was the difficulty I had in town with the Leslie boys that started it." He told Pritchard of the argument, and how the Negro police had thrown them in jail.

After he finished, Pritchard said, "My son, Nixon, had Ed Leslie in his company. A good man, although I don't know him personally. And good of you, suh, to see an injustice and right it." He folded his hands. "But you didn't come here to tell me about that."

"No, sir," Heinz said. "General, Texas is poor and the little money the Union army is spending here is a drop in the bucket. If Texas doesn't do something soon, the money from the north will start coming this way, buying everything it can, and before you know it—"

"I'm well aware of that, suh," Pritchard said. "When it comes, it'll be war all over again."

"General, it would be better to avoid that," Heinz said. "Texas has a product to sell: cattle. The range is glutted with cattle."

"Yes, and a market sixteen hundred miles away, in St. Louis." He shook his head. "Mr. Heinz, I've talked myself hoarse on the matter. We couldn't drive a herd that far, with hostile Indians and—"

"General, I believe there's a market a thousand miles away, in Kansas. He leaned forward and there was a new excitement in his voice. "We passed through Kansas and there's a tent city springing up there, right at the end of the railroad. I talked to some men there who were buyers of cattle, and they had their eye on Texas but there was no way to reach those herds.

No way to bring cattle and railroad together."

"A drive of a thousand miles has never been attempted," Pritchard said. "Why, it would take eight months." He shook his head. "And I don't know of anyone with enough money to stake such a drive. It would take five hundred dollars to buy the supplies just to make the drive." Then his eyes narrowed. "Then too, I have only your word that this tent city exists. Has it a name?"

"Yes. Abilene. Abilene, Kansas."

Pritchard thought about it. "Even if it is true, no one has the money to—"

"General, could you get a herd together?"

"Yes, nearly five thousand head."

"Then I can get the money," Heinz said. "General, I have some money of my own, not much, a little over four hundred dollars. And I know officers on the post who like a good investment. We'll put up the money, and take one dollar a head for every one that is sold in Abilene. By your count, sir."

"That's a fat profit," Pritchard said frankly.

"Yes, it is," Heinz said. "Also big risks. We don't know if such a thing can even be done. We're gambling on each other, sir. I think I can raise twelve hundred dollars. You get the herd together and the men to drive them. As I recall, the market price at Abilene ran about thirty dollars a head. That's about a hundred and fifty thousand dollars, general. My share would amount to about five thousand. Drovers' expenses, wages, and so forth for eight months would come to approximately twenty-five thousand dollars. Paid in Abilene, of course; it would have to be a condition of the drive."

"I think those figures are about right," Pritchard said.

"I'm not quite finished, sir," Heinz said. "We don't stop with one herd. As soon as one is on the trail, we'll put together another."

"Man, I don't have that many cattle," Pritchard said.

"Not your cattle, general, but other men's cattle. I am proposing that we go into the drover business. Remember, I was at Abilene. I made the march south to Texas and I can map out the trail. The two of us can finance the drives and take a larger share, say five dollars a head."

Nan said, "I've always heard that Yankees were opportunists. I guess it's true."

He looked at her. "If your father doesn't do this, some other man will, and he may not be a Texan. Someone is surely going to do this. When that first herd reaches Abilene, there are men there who are going to see the merits of this idea, get into a wagon, and start south."

Pritchard said, "Mr. Heinz, when I gather a herd and start a drive, others will do the same. There'll be no stopping that."

"Yes, but your trail boss will know the way.

The others will be firing blind. Some may make it, but it will be a year before they can get back and pass the information along."

"It seems like an underhanded thing to do," Pritchard said.

"General, there's more to lose than you think. You give the police another year and they'll have enough laws passed in Texas to make it a crime to own a firearm. And then when you can't protect yourself, the Yankee opportunists will come here like a plague and strip you clean."

"Strange," Nan said, "to hear a man say that, when he once wore the same uniform—"

"You're mistaken," Heinz said flatly. "The officers commanding the police are not army and never served. They're political appointments of men who held reserve commissions in state militia units. The uniforms were issued because the government had plenty of them. You won't find a soldier at the post who has any love or respect for the police." He looked at Pritchard. "General, you fought a war and lost, and you know why the south lost. Those factories in the north, and the money in the north out produced you. The last two years, your men got hungrier and poorer and the Union army got stronger. Look at Texas, general, like a steer on its back, waiting for someone to come along and strip the hide off it."

Nathan Pritchard nodded solemnly. "Yes, that's true." He looked at Heinz, his white, bushy eyebrows bunched. "I don't think you really need me at all. With money in your hand, you could have put a herd together by yourself and named your own price."

"I thought of that, general," Heinz said frankly. "But it wouldn't be any good. Texas needs a leader, and you've been that leader in this part of the lick for many years. Take her out of her troubles, general. I don't want the job."

"That's very flattering," Pritchard said. "And sincerely said." He extended his hand. "I seal my bargains in this manner. Will you honor that, suh?"

"Of course," Heinz said and stood up. "I've taken you from your reading, general. My apologies."

Pritchard laughed. "I have more than a book to interest me now. Will you be my guest? We have much to talk about in the weeks to come."

"I'm with the Leslie boys—"

"When I invite a man," Pritchard said, "I include his horse and his friends."

"Thank you, general. That's appreciated."

"Nan, have one of the servants summon Nix and Owen," he said and they left the library. He waited in the hall while she spoke to a servant, then she came over to him.

"I really can't quite make you out, Mr. Heinz."

"My name is Carl."

"All right, Carl. Would you care to explain something to me?"

"If I can?"

"Tell me why you resigned from the army."

He smiled and scratched his head. "It's rather involved, and it has to do with what a man believes or doesn't believe. The military governs Texas. That in itself doesn't seem so bad since Texas can't govern herself yet. But there are too many laws being passed, too many restrictions being placed on Texans. And I'm not sure the army knows how to do the job. But I don't want to bore you with policy."

"I won't be," she said.

"All right, Colonel Shannon is to clean up Texas and make it fit for settlers. I don't like that. Of course, they'll come, but on Texas terms, not on their own, with the way paved by the politics of Washington. Colonel Shannon is to subdue the outlaw element. Of course it has to be subdued, but who are these men who rob banks and stages and steal cattle? There is little money in the banks and the stages are poor pickings and the cattle are eaten, not sold. This leads me to believe that these men are more desperate than lawless."

"We've learned not to expect sympathy from the north," Nan said. "Can you blame us?"

"Yes," Heinz said. "It's difficult for me to understand how a people who are so proud of their traditions and principles can be so mistrustful of it in others."

"I suppose it does look that way, doesn't it?" She bit her lower lip. "But we lost the war and we expect to be punished. We don't want to be, but we expect it nevertheless."

"If the settlers and the fast dollar investors ever hit this country," Heinz said, "you'll be punished. They'll buy you for a dollar and throw you clear out of Texas."

"Father says that's already happening in the south."

"It is. The only thing that's holding them back now is distance," Heinz said. "We're not going to stop them, Nan. I don't think there is a power on earth that can stop exploitation, but we can slow them down when they get here. Money will do that. Texas has to have money in her jeans when they come here."

4

The next morning, Carl Heinz rode to the post and tied up by headquarters. The noon mess was letting out and he went into Lieutenant Malcolm's office to wait for his return. He came in, and smiled, surprised to find Heinz there.

"Get lone-some already?" Malcolm asked.

"I came to get my money from the paymaster," Heinz said. "Is the colonel in to sign the release slip?"

"He'll be back soon," Malcolm said. "What have you been up to? Captain Dane is hopping mad."

"Is he on the post?"

"No, he left this morning. He's putting a poster out on you, that's what."

Shannon's step crossed the porch and he stepped in and stopped when he saw Heinz. "I want a word with you, *Mister* Heinz."

"And I want to talk to you, colonel. I want to get my money out of the paymaster's safe."

Shannon glanced at Malcolm. "Make out the slip and I'll sign it. Come into the office, Carl. Close the door." He sat down behind his desk. "I had a long talk with Dane and got nowhere. Damn it, what did you bail those two toughs out for? Dane wanted to hold them."

"Then why was bail set?"

Shannon waved his hand. "Hell, he knows no one has the money to go bail."

Heinz smiled. "He must have been surprised."

"Surprised? He was foaming at the mouth. Both of those men came to town to rob the bank, or at least that's what the rumor going around leads Dane to believe. Besides, they held up a store two weeks ago, stole some flour and beans and two plugs of tobacco." He shook his finger at Heinz. "Dane's putting out a poster on you. How do you like that?"

"I don't give a damn," Heinz said. "No one pays any attention to his posters."

"Except the police," Shannon said. "Look, go to Marfa and see Dane. Square this somehow.

You don't want to be mixed up with these riff-raff."

Malcolm knocked and came in with the paymaster's slip. "Three thousand and eight dollars, sir," he said and laid it on Shannon's desk for the signature. Then he took the slip. "I'll get your money," he said and went out.

"Carl, that money's been drawing three per cent," Shannon said. "Six years in the saving." He frowned. "A man carrying that kind of money may not live long."

"Hell, colonel, a man with no money at all may not live long."

Shannon shrugged. "Well, it's a point. Got something in mind?"

"A little business deal," Heinz said. He wasn't about to talk about it to Shannon any more than he was going to tell General Pritchard that he had that much money; the general would naturally distrust him if he waved that kind of a bankroll.

"Well, I hope you don't lose your shirt," Shannon said. "And Carl, see Paul Dane. Don't get off on the wrong foot with the authorities."

"I intend to see Dane," Heinz said, "but not for the reason you think."

He went out to wait for Malcolm, and it wasn't long. The money was in gold and Malcolm put it in a canvas moneybelt which Heinz fastened under his shirt. Then he mounted up and left the post, taking the Marfa road.

There was no use, he decided, in riding the

39

horse into the ground to make it by sundown, so he set a relaxed pace and arrived late at night. The saloon sported lights, and the jail, and that was all, so he put his horse in the stable, crawled into the loft and bedded down in the hay.

The town was quiet, except for occasional horsemen riding up and down the street, and Heinz figured these would be police patrols. He fell asleep and woke with the sound of men yelling and they sounded like Negro police, then a rifle went off, the boom of it echoing through the stillness of the night. Heinz got up and went to the loft door and looked out; he could see the street, or a good part of it, and there were police running around with lanterns and orders being shouted, then they came toward the barn on the run.

Below, the door opened and closed and he could hear a man's heavy breathing and Heinz stirred and sifted some dust down for the man said, "Who's that?"

"They after you?" Heinz asked. He couldn't make out the man, other than a smudged shadow by the door. The police were getting closer and there wasn't any time to debate this thing. "Are you armed?"

"Wish to God I was," the man said fervently. "They'll kill me without a trial."

Good sense told him not to do it but this was a desperate time and he unbuckled his gunbelt, rolled it around the holster and dropped it. The man picked it up and Heinz said, "Out the back. My horse is in the last stall."

"Bless you, stranger," the man said and was gone. He was clear of the barn and the town by the time the first police arrived and they came into the barn with their noise and lanterns and Heinz looked down from the loft at them.

"What's goin' on?" he asked.

A nervous man flung a shot at him and they came up the ladder and shined lanterns in his face and a black sergeant with large white eyeballs said, "He not de one. You. Where he go?"

"Where did who go? What's the idea waking a man from a sound sleep?"

"You come wid us," the sergeant said and they took him down from the loft and marched him down the street to the police office.

A few minutes later Captain Dane came in. He was a slight man with thinning hair and a pair of gold-rimmed glasses pinched to his thin nose. He looked at Heinz, then peered closer, then swore. "What are you doing here, Heinz?"

"Ask the sergeant," Heinz said. "He brought me here."

Dane swung to the man. "This isn't Hardin. You damned fool, Hardin's a boy, barely sixteen years old."

"Ah know dat, suh, but we had Hardin. He got away, suh. Ran in de barn, den we foun' dis gennimans."

"Oh, you blasted idiots," Dane said and for a moment, Heinz thought he was going to strike the man. Then he calmed himself "What were you doing in the barn, Heinz?"

"Sleeping."

"There's a hotel."

"It was dark," Heinz said. "Have you got a law against sleeping in the barn?"

Dane blew out an irritated breath. "I suppose you heard nothing?"

"Well, I heard all the yelling as your men came in, then I was hauled down from the loft. Wait now. Someone rode out on a horse. I think that's what woke me. Say! My horse——"

Dane said, "Sergeant, go see if Mr. Heinz's horse is gone." He sat down and rubbed his eyes. "I want Hardin and I'll get him. He killed a police officer who was only performing his duty." Then he looked at Heinz. "If I can prove you had anything to do with his getting away——"

"You go right ahead and try," Heinz said flatly. "I hear you're getting a poster out on me."

"Because you're interfering in the discharge of my affairs," Dane snapped. "Heinz, my duty is clear to me. By the time I'm through, Texas will be cleaned out of these lawless elements."

"Your dedication staggers me," Heinz said, and Dane missed the point. He sat down and Dane frowned and it pleased Heinz to see this man's vanity pricked. "I rode here to talk to you, captain. Don't put my name up on walls."

"If I see fit—"

"I've told you to be careful!" Heinz snapped and Dane's eyes widened. "God, man, are you so stupid you can't see I mean it? Has authority so crowded your head that you can't tell when you're overstepping yourself? You pompous little ass, I was a soldier when you were keeping books for some war profiteer. Don't push me or I'll drive you in the ground and use you for a fence post."

Heinz turned to the door and Dane said, "I haven't discharged you yet!"

"I've discharged myself," Heinz said and stepped out. There was little he could do; he was without a horse or a gun and he didn't want to hang around town while Dane mulled this over in his mind.

Still he didn't want to chance it on the prairie without a horse or a gun. Without attracting any attention, he went back to the stable and found no one there. There were some horses in the corral in back, but to take one would be a hanging offense.

He was stuck with the town and didn't like it, but it wasn't the first thing in his life that he hadn't liked. The alleys were safer than the street, so he went behind the saloon, moving carefully not to crash into the piled boxes and beer barrels.

Then a door opened suddenly and Heinz was caught in a blare of lamplight partially blocked by a man. He stopped and the man said, "You're the fella in the barn, ain't you? Come inside." He stepped aside and Heinz went in and the man closed the door. They were in a storeroom and there was a small office to one side. The man was round in the belly, but not soft, and he stood a half a head taller than Heinz. He led the way to the office and said, "Want a drink?"

"I can use one," Heinz admitted and took the glass. It was good stuff, private stock, and he turned the glass upside down when he was through, indicating that he had had enough.

"The name's Pete Burgess. Hardin is a friend of mine. Knew the family well." He looked at Heinz. "Where's your gun?"

"Who said I had one?"

"You got wrinkles in your pants where a gun-belt sat," Burgess said. "You goin' to tell me?"

"I gave it to Hardin," Heinz said. "He took my horse too."

"You know Hardin then?"

"Wouldn't know him if I saw him," Heinz admitted.

Burgess frowned. "You gave him your gun and horse, then lied to Dane?"

"I don't like Dane," Heinz said. "Law and order I'm for, but not the kind where one person makes the laws, the arrests, and does the hanging."

"I'll get you another gun and a horse," Burgess said. "You wait here." He went out and Heinz sat down and waited and then Burgess came back with a Navy Colt and some paper cartridges in a wooden box. "You go to the west end of town and there'll be a horse waitin' for you. He ain't much because the police rounded up most of the good horses, but he'll take you where you're goin', if you ain't goin' far."

"To Pritchard's," Heinz said.

Burgess nodded. "You travel in good company."

"Depends on the point of view," Heinz said. "Dane wouldn't agree with you."

"He may not live long," Burgess said. "And some of his men got a short life only they don't know it."

"This can't last forever," Heinz said. "What happened to the law Texas used to have?"

Burgess shrugged. "They're around, but they can't do anything. The police have all the authority. We ain't supposed to go around armed, you know. So you keep that gun under your coat."

"Thanks," Heinz said and went out into the alley again.

He walked to the west end of town and found a man standing there with a horse. The man said nothing and Heinz mounted up and swung out, moving along the road but keeping an ear tuned to the sound of a police patrol.

He figured they'd be out in numbers because Hardin was a wanted man and they wouldn't give up easily, and he supposed that someone might get killed before dawn broke.

45

But he really didn't care. In this country, the way things were, a man had all he could do to keep a watch over himself and let the next man have his own worries.

Dawn found him tired and dusty and thirty miles out of Paul Dane's reach, and when he got to town he stopped for a drink, then went to the general store. The owner was sweeping down the place and he put his broom aside when Heinz went to the counter.

"This afternoon," Heinz said, "I want you to go to the Pritchard place. Bring your pencil and paper to take a large order."

"I got to go by cash," the man said regretfully.

Heinz bumped his stomach against the counter so the man could hear the gold. "That's what I'm talking about. Cash. You be there."

"I'll be there," he said and Heinz left the store. He knew this would stir talk and he wanted it to because these people needed something to hope for and the thought that maybe the Pritchards had raised some money would be a boost to them. It had to be that way because the Pritchards made the county, and in a way, were the county. If Pritchard could give his Texans something to think about, something real to work on, maybe there'd be fewer excuses for Dane and his misled police to latch onto.

When he dismounted in the Pritchard yard, a man took the horse to the barn while Heinz went on to the house. He found Nan and her sister in the main hall, supervising the servants at their weekly cleaning.

Cecilia Pritchard was older than Nan by two years and a striking woman in an aloof, proud way. She looked at the dust on Heinz's clothes and the stubble on his face and was repelled by it. Nan was not.

She said, "I used to have a cat like you; never would stay in at night, and one night he never came back."

Heinz grinned. "There's a moral to that, someplace. But it was an exciting night. Is your father here?"

"Don't you ever want to see anyone else?"

"Nan!" Cecilia snapped. "Excuse me." She flounced out of the hall and they watched her go.

"She's very proper," Nan said, smiling. "Father's outside with Nix and Owen. They were gone half the night. Father's going to have a meeting here today."

"About the cattle?"

"Yes. I hope you haven't raised his hopes too high about the money."

He tapped the belt. "It's here. Now what's left over from breakfast?"

5

Colonel Race Daniels was General Pritchard's nearest neighbor, and he came to the meeting, and two other cattlemen with smaller outfits, and they talked in the library and pretty much agreed with everything the general said. Daniels was not completely sold on the notion of working with a Yankee, but he could see the necessity of having some money, and he had practically none at all.

The storekeeper came and was given an order, which caused him to write excitedly; it would take three wagons to deliver it, and nearly nine hundred dollars to pay for it, and this money was counted out and promised when the barrels and boxes and bags arrived at Pritchard's store-house.

After the storekeeper went back to town, Pritchard outlined his plans for getting the drive started. He would ship three thousand head and his two sons, Nixon and Owen would head the drive. Daniels would add a thousand head to this, with the smaller ranchers making up a thousand head between them. Manpower was not a problem; there were more men than jobs and any man who completed the drive got his pay plus a bonus which he could take back to Texas and live on for a year, and live well. Horses would be a problem, but Daniels figured the best way to get them would be in the Indian country and Carl Heinz agreed to head up the horse gathering; Daniels figured they'd need four hundred horses, a figure he mentioned casually, but which caused Heinz to swallow hard.

General Pritchard, never a man to bivouac when he could advance, claimed that four weeks ought to be enough time, and ended the meeting by announcing that the herd would move at that time. After they had mounted their buggies and driven off, Nathan Pritchard was in an expansive mood; he poured two whiskeys and settled in his favorite chair.

"Mr. Heinz, you've given us hope, the kind a working man can sink his teeth into." He raised his glass and nodded. "I am also kinder disposed to these Yankees for their loans of money."

"Love and profit, general, are both strong motives."

"Indeed," Pritchard said. "I can give you twenty men on the horse gathering. Daniels can come up with ten and a man who knows the country. Had we more time, we might trade for horses, but I'm afraid they'll either have to be stolen or gathered from wild herds. And since this is not wild horse country—"

"I understand, general," Heinz said. "We'll get the horses."

"A pity the police took our best stock," Pritchard

said idly. "They have more than they can use, you know."

"I'll look into it," Heinz said. "If you'll tell your foreman that I'd like to leave in the morning—"

"That will be taken care of," Pritchard said. "I believe my daughter likes the south veranda, Mr. Heinz. Something about the morning sun."

This was, Heinz knew, as polite a dismissal as he'd get and he left the study and walked down the long hall, but left the house by a side entrance and cut across the wide yard to the bunkhouse.

Ed and Joe Leslie were there, mending saddles. Heinz said, "See if you can scrape up a wagon and a team."

"We goin' someplace?" Joe asked.

"Naw," Ed said, "he's just never seen a wagon and a team before." He slapped his cousin playfully on the head and they went out.

Heinz waited in the yard and then Nixon Pritchard walked over. He was a quiet, withdrawn man who spoke sparingly and smiled even less. "What do you want with a wagon, Mr. Heinz?"

"I thought I'd try to get us some repeating rifles," Heinz said. "I've been noticing that most every-one has either a cavalry pistol or a muzzle-loading carbine."

"We got what was left over from the war," Nix said. "Ain't there a sayin': beggars can't be choosers?"

Heinz ignored the bitterness in the man. "I

know that Colonel Shannon has three cases of Henry repeating rifles in the ordnance shed. They were issued to him because no one wanted them. They're .44 rimfire and don't shoot much farther than a good pistol, but you can load them on Sunday and shoot all week. I'm going to try to get them."

Nix Pritchard grinned. "By golly now—"

Heinz slapped him on the arm. "I'll see what I can do."

Ed and his cousin came across the yard with the wagon and Heinz got aboard and they rattled away. He stood behind the seat, knees bent to take up the eternal jolt and rattle.

What a miserable way to travel, Heinz thought, and marveled that anyone had ever crossed a continent in wagons. Ed Leslie drove with a touch of madness; he liked lively horses and seemed immune to bumps and several times he got the rear wheels of the wagon six inches off the ground.

At the post, the sentry admitted them and Heinz had Leslie park by headquarters while he went inside. Lieutenant Malcolm ushered him into Colonel Shannon's office and Shannon said, "What are you going to do, call on me every day, Carl?"

"No, sir," Heinz said. "Colonel, I came to talk to you about the Henry rifles in the ordnance shed."

"What about them?"

"I'd like to buy them, sir, and any of the other

51

arms designated surplus. When I was adjutant, sir, I recall a directive—"

"Yes, yes," Shannon said, waving his hand. "But if you think I'm going to release those rifles just like that—" He snapped his fingers.

"Colonel, in a few weeks, General Pritchard is going to make a cattle drive to the northern market," Heinz said. "They'll be eight months on the trail, through Indian country and Lord knows what. I think they deserve something better than Confederate muzzle-loaders."

"Carl, I can't arm the Texans. You know that's against the law."

"But you could assign the weapons to me, sir."

"I'd have to hold you responsible for anything that happened," Shannon said, shaking his head. "Of course, I only inventory once a year. No, it's out of the question."

Heinz smiled. "Colonel, as an ex-officer I'm privileged to buy surplus equipment for my own purposes. I would like to make application, sir."

"Damn it, don't put me on the spot like that," Shannon said, spreading his hands in an appeal. "I'm in sympathy with you, but this is arming the Texans and the law—"

"Violation of Captain Dane's laws would be my concern, wouldn't it?" He bravely leaned on Shannon's desk, a thing he had never done before. "Colonel, you hate his guts and always have. You don't care what he thinks, or about his puny laws."

"Now I'm not going to admit that," Shannon said.

"Do you deny it then?"

"I'm not going to do that either," he said and drew a piece of paper to him and scrawled a note. "All right, buy what you want. But, Carl, you're getting in deep."

Heinz left the building and walked to the ordnance shed, motioning for Ed and Joe Leslie to come along with the wagon. Lieutenant Malcolm left headquarters with a ring of brass keys and he opened the heavy door.

"Going to start a little war of your own?" Malcolm asked. He opened some oak shutters that closed off the barred windows, letting in light; powder was stored in there and they couldn't risk a lantern.

Malcolm opened the boxes containing the Henry repeaters and Heinz inspected them; they were almost new and many had been unfired. He counted sixty, then turned to Malcolm. "How much ammunition do you have for these rifles?"

"A wooden carton per crate, Carl. About eighteen thousand rounds." He did some mental arithmetic. "Three hundred rounds per man."

"We'll take the whole lot," Carl Heinz said. "Ed, Joe, come in here and carry these boxes to the wagon." He turned to Malcolm. "As I recall, you had some .44 Starr revolvers here."

"Yes, a case of fifty," Malcolm said. "I'll bet

the old man will give them to you to get rid of them; he considers them heavy, clumsy, and completely unsuited for military duty." He pointed to another box. "There's linen cartridges enough to fight the battle of Shiloh over. They're yours."

"Ed, take these along too," Heinz said, pointing to the crates.

Heinz looked around. "What ever happened to those breech-loading Sharps carbines the 16th Ohio Cavalry foisted off on us?" He smiled at Malcolm. "The old man never liked those either."

They were loaded and the Leslie boys were working up a sweat and as Malcolm locked the ordnance shed, Ed whispered, "Let's get out of here before someone changes their mind."

"We're not stealing them," Heinz said and went with Malcolm to headquarters. Colonel Shannon could set the price; it was within his authority to dispose of unwanted equipment as he saw fit. He charged Heinz junk price, thirty-five dollars, which was paid, a receipt pocketed, and Heinz got in the wagon and they drove off the post.

After they cleared the gate, the Leslie boys looked at each other, then Joe said, "I don't believe it. We got guns."

Ed nodded. "And we got trouble if we run into a patrol of police too."

"The guns are mine," Heinz said. "And I'm

54

allowed to own firearms." He patted them on the back and laughed. "Drive on, boys."

At the Pritchard ranch house the wagon was backed to the west wing of the porch and the cases unloaded and stacked against the wall. Nathan Pritchard came out and Heinz said, "General, would you call all the hands, please?"

"Are those rifles, suh?" Heinz nodded and Pritchard motioned to one of the Leslie boys who immediately went out to the well and beat on a metal triangle with a shovel. Men came from the barn and the bunkhouse and corrals and even the cookshack where they'd been sneaking a cup of coffee; at least sixty gathered around the porch and watched the crates being opened.

Leaned against the wall, they displayed the rifles and revolvers very handily and it caused a lot of talk, which quieted when Heinz held up his hands.

"Tomorrow morning some of you are riding with me into the Indian country after horses," Heinz said. "When you do, you'll be wearing a good percussion pistol at your belt and a new repeater across the saddle." This started a buzz of excited talk.

Pritchard said, "Quiet! Ain't you got no manners?"

"You all know the law Captain Dane's put into effect about owning firearms," Heinz said. "All right, each man is going to get a piece of paper saying that the firearms he carries do not belong to him, but have been loaned." He looked at Nathan Pritchard. "Perhaps, sir, your daughters could be persuaded to write out the documents."

"They will, I assure you," Pritchard said.

The men were still listening, so Heinz went on with his explanation. "Now we don't want to break Dane's damned law, and we won't. Of course he'll be mad as hell when he finds out, but some of us will be in Indian country and likely we'll be on the move north with the herd before he can change the law."

Heinz had heard the rebel yell before, but under less happy circumstances; these men danced and whooped and threw hats in the air and he had trouble getting them quiet. Nan and Cecilia came out to see what all this was about, and their presence brought order.

"Now these guns and ammunition are not free," Heinz said. "To get them you sign up for the horse hunt or the cattle drive. When you get back, or when we reach the railhead, they're yours. And not before."

One lanky man said, "Mister if'n ah hunt horses, do ah get a gun?"

"That's right."

"And if'n ah go noath, do ah get another."

"You get another rifle," Heinz said. "There aren't enough revolvers to go around."

"Why, then, you all jus' put me down fer two," the man said and everyone laughed.

"As soon as the papers are written up, you can draw your guns," Heinz said. "General, if a small table could be brought out here, I'll take the names of the men as they're issued and—"

"Of course, suh. Nan, will you have one of the servants tend to it?"

Another man said, "Mistah Heinz, if'n it ain't too much bothah, could we see some shootin' by one of them repeatah's?"

"If you drinking men will line up some empty whiskey bottles on that corral fence over there." He pointed. "Eighteen will do it."

"Man, do it hold that many shots?" one asked.

While they got the bottles, he selected a Henry repeater at random, but took one that had been fired, figuring that the former owner had already made his adjustments to the sights, and loaded it. He waited while the bottles were placed, then quickly shouldered the piece and rapidly broke all eighteen of them.

It was a bit of show off shooting on his part, but he thought it was necessary because the right impression was necessary and he formed a line to the porch and threatened trouble if there was any fighting for a place in it.

"You spread the word quietly about this now," he said and turned to find Cecilia Pritchard watching him.

"I didn't think you could break them all," she said. "You were lucky."

He smiled. "No credit for skill?"

"All right then. You're a dead shot. You're also an extremely clever man. Almost sly."

"I prefer clever," Heinz said. "What are we going to do, fight?"

"It would be silly, wouldn't it?" she said. "I wish I could trust you. I want to, you know."

"Do you?" He took her arm and led her to one side. "Cecilia, let's understand something right now. I'm doing what I believe in, because I believe in it. If I'm rude to you, or appear to ignore you, I'm sorry, but I just don't have time to waste on being courtly."

He thought she was going to slap his face; she raised her palm then thought better of it and wheeled away, almost bumping into Nan. She stepped gingerly aside, then said, "What's the matter with her?"

"War," he said.

"War my foot. Cecilia's just not getting her own way."

6

Captain Paul Dane did not feel particularly secure unless he had a twelve man patrol behind him, and with this force he toured the prairie looking for trouble. General Pritchard's buildings were in the distance when he halted and listened to the sound of gunfire.

Then he altered his course and rode toward the Pritchard place at a gallop.

Carl Heinz saw the dust and made them out first, and he quickly gave his orders. "No loading of the firearms! Continue to hand them out, Nan." He turned to the general. "With your permission, sir, I'll talk with Captain Dane."

"Granted," Pritchard said. "I loathe the man myself."

When Dane came into the yard and saw the rifles, he spread his detail in a line and came on to the porch with drawn weapons. "You are all under arrest," he announced. "You too, Heinz."

"Arrested for what?" Heinz asked. Everyone had stopped and he motioned for them to go ahead.

"You know it's against the law for Texans to have firearms," Dane said. "You've gone too far this time."

"The law says that it's illegal for them to own firearms," Heinz said calmly. "If you'll look at the pieces of paper being issued, you'll see that the firearms are being loaned. No one here has broken the law."

"By God, you can't use trickery to evade the law!" Dane shouted. "I can change the law, you know."

"Then change it," Heinz said. "But it'll take time. You'll have to draw up the amendment, submit it to Colonel Shannon for approval and then enforce it. That'll take you a month anyway because the colonel's heavy on paperwork." He waved his hands. "You take your police and get out of here. Start trouble and you'll wish you'd brought along another thirty men." He pointed to the Texans. "Count the rifles, Dane. Can you shoot your way out of this? I don't think you can and I don't think you have the guts for it if you could."

This was the truth and Dane knew it but he had to rage a bit. "Heinz, I'm going to see you in jail if it's the last thing I ever do." He motioned to his sergeant and they wheeled and left the yard.

General Pritchard sighed and said, "Close, suh, mighty close."

"He's gunshy," Heinz said and went on issuing rifles and revolvers.

At dawn he left, with twenty men, and rode to Race Daniels' place, picked up another sixteen men, then headed across open country to an outflung corner of Daniels' ranch where he kept a line camp going all year around.

This was to be the gathering place for the wagons and the rest of the men and from there they'd push west and north into the Indian country for the horses.

The word had gotten out and after they made camp by the few buildings, riders streamed in, sometimes in pairs, sometimes alone. A few came by the half dozen until there were sixty men there.

The cooking was done on big firepits with the chuck wagons backed up and parked side by side and the grub line formed on both sides for this was one outfit, a common effort from here on in.

The new men were curious about the shiny Henry repeaters and many of them came up to Heinz and gave him their names so they could get one when they got back. He carefully wrote the names in a small notebook, not really paying any attention to the faces.

Then a man gave him his name and he looked up. "Hardin?" he said.

"I said Hardin."

He was slender, not fully filled out and his face was smooth, one of those shaved twice a month faces. Heinz said, "I'll take my pistol and belt back now."

Hardin stiffened, then said, "Who says I got it?"

"I do," Heinz said. "I tossed it down from the hay loft and gave you my horse."

The men standing around heard this and grew quiet and Hardin relaxed and laughed. "Wondered if I'd ever meet you again." He unbuckled the belt and handed it to Carl Heinz. "I thank you for the loan of it. It shoots good."

Heinz took the belt and handed Hardin the Navy Colt. "A loan from Pete Burgess. You might give it back the next time you see him."

"It's my kind of gun," Hardin said and stuck it in his waistband. "You know who I am?"

"Dane says you killed a policeman," Heinz said.

"I shot another since I left that barn," Hardin said. "Didn't kill him though." He squatted and tapped Carl Heinz on the knee. "Mister, you couldn't even see me. How come you gave me your gun and horse?"

"You sounded like a man who'd run to the end of the string," Heinz said.

"How come a Yankee like you is headin' up this outfit?"

"Because I decided to," Heinz told him. "You've asked enough questions now."

"Well, I ain't made up my mind to that yet," Hardin said.

"I have," Heinz said. "Now go get another helping of beans."

Hardin stood up slowly and said, "I don't know as I want to work for a Yankee."

"Suit yourself. No work, no repeater." He tipped his head back and looked at the young man. "And Hardin, I'd say you need the repeater because you've got the looks of a shooting man, real wild in the eye and on edge all the time. Do you want your name to stay in my book or do I scratch it out? Make up your mind because there's fellas behind you waiting."

"Leave it in," Hardin said and went to the cook's fire.

The line finally ended and Ed Leslie came over and hunkered down. "You pushed Hardin kind of hard, Carl. I never knew him to take much of that."

"Known him long?"

"Long enough to know he's plumb wild," Ed Leslie said. "You might have been smarter if you'd not given him the gun and horse." He took a bite of cut plug. "One of these days he's goin' to find out that Texans is as easy to shoot as police."

Behind them now was four days of riding, and ahead was another four and they saw their first herd of wild horses on the sixth and made camp to spend a week in that one place, ranging out for twenty miles, working the herd in shifts until it was about run out, and only then could they begin to put a rope on the horses. In all, they captured a hundred and twenty and these were hurriedly broken to lead rope, and twenty-five men remained with the herd while Heinz and the others moved on.

The men who stayed had a job to do, a tough, mean job of getting the horses back to Pritchard's place where they'd be broken to some half wild state and picked by the riders.

Heinz kept wondering where the Indians were for this was their section of prairie, and he suspected they were around because the Texans were ever watchful, and a little nervous at night.

Wild horse sign was about and he decided to establish another camp with the remaining wagon and range out, for they were against a good river and wood was handy and if they had to fight, this was a good place to do it.

In camp he always kept ten men; the others were sent out, in all directions, to look for a horse herd. For three days Heinz waited in camp, but no one came back, and this really didn't worry him; he wouldn't start worrying for another four days because he knew a horse hunt could take a man a lot of miles before he found anything.

Ed and Joe Leslie stayed in the main camp as part of the guard, and they kept watching the far horizons and the rises and even built themselves a nest in one of the taller trees so they could have a better look.

Ed's signal, when it came, was a low whistle, and he pointed to a distant rise and every man could see the Indians sitting their horses, about sixty or seventy strong and decked out in all their ferocious paint.

"Comanch," Joe Leslie said. "No talk. Fight. They ain't the talkin' kind."

"Then I guess we'll fight," Heinz said and checked the magazine in his rifle. "How do they attack, Joe?"

"In a charge," Leslie said. "I'd hold off though until they got in close. If you don't break the charge they're liable to run right over us."

"Can we beat 'em off?" Heinz asked.

Joe Leslie grinned. "If we don't our hair's goin'

to be hangin' on one of their lances come night-fall." He spat tobacco. "They only got a few trade muskets, but man, you ought to see 'em ride and shoot arrors. Oops. Here they come."

They were sound, thunder and yelling and a storm racing off the rise and the Texans let them come on, to a hundred and fifty yards, and to a hundred, then the Henry repeaters began to snap and riders dropped and it was as if nothing happened for they did not break stride, but kept on coming and Heinz worked the lever of his rifle and poured shot after shot into them.

But they broke a scant distance from the line of Texans and they were so close that one Indian fell into their midst and had to be pushed away to give them room.

Even wheeling away, the Indians were under constant fire, then they drew out of decent range and Carl Heinz had time to look around. He saw two men dead and Ed Leslie with a bleeding arm and he hadn't realized that the Indians had been firing at all. Arrows stuck in the side of the wagon and in the ground and out of the two dead men.

Ed Leslie said, "Rough game. Here they come again."

It seemed incredible to Heinz that they'd charge again after so severe a loss, but they were coming and he hadn't even reloaded his rifle. He worked the catch under the barrel and began to insert shells and the firing began while he was still at it, then he got his rifle charged and began shooting.

He could see the arrows now and it was a nerve-wracking thing to watch them fly in an arc, seemingly pointed right at him, then have them land a few feet away; one went through his coat sleeve and pinned his arm to the ground. He jerked it free, breaking the arrow, and went on shooting.

It seemed as though the Indians would never stop coming, and there was so much noise that he could not hear his own Henry go off; he knew it was firing because there was a mild kick at his shoulder and he could see the black powder smoke.

At last the Indians broke away, passing on either side and reforming and Heinz thought, God, not another attack! They rode back up the hill, or part way, and there they stopped and for a moment Heinz could not understand their hesitation, then he heard a low rumble, a drumming sound like distant thunder, and Ed Leslie yelled, "Stampede! Stampede!"

What stampede? Heinz thought, then he saw the horse herd crest the rise and bore full tilt into the Indians. And the Indians left in a hurry while the horses came on, flanked by the Texans.

How they got the animals turned and milling before they went into the river Heinz never understood, but then he was always amazed at the Texans' ability to handle beasts.

Quieting the horse herd and getting them under control took the rest of the day and the better part of the night and the fire was kept going until daylight and the cook worked his helpers in shifts to be sure there was always biscuits and beans and coffee hot.

The Indians were gone, but their dead remained, nearly thirty, some of them badly mangled by the horses as they had milled; Heinz had some men shovel them under and the Texans didn't like this, but they did it anyway.

All of the men who'd left on the horse hunt didn't come back; one because he was dead, and another, young Hardin, because he'd killed the man and taken off. Heinz had lost two men in the Indian attack and they were buried and quickly forgotten by the Texans; all they wanted to talk about was the horses they'd taken and how good these repeaters were in a fight.

It was a way of thinking completely different from anything Carl Heinz had known, for when an officer lost men, he had to come up with a pretty good reason, or find himself in trouble. His commanding officer wouldn't like it and the men wouldn't like it for it was hell to serve under a careless or stupid officer.

There were some wounded men, but they could ride, and at dawn they broke camp along the river and started back, using up each day to trail break the horses.

The Texans were leather; they not only rode from dawn to dark, but at night fashioned rope corrals and broke as many horses as they could. This was done at some cost for one man broke a leg and three more had arm fractures while one lanky man kept hurting a knee that had never healed from an earlier injury.

It was a hard life, a dangerous one, and there was no sympathy for any man who couldn't stick on the horse he'd elected to ride. Exactly twenty-three days from the time they left Pritchard's ranch, Heinz once again saw the buildings and the Pritchard clan rode out to meet them, the men on horseback, the two girls in buggies.

The general was pleased and had cigars and some whiskey to pass around. Then he drew Heinz aside. "I told my sons here you'd be back within thirty days. We've not wasted our time either, suh." He motioned to the south where the earth seemed a solid brown flecked by an occasional touch of white. "Nigh onto six thousand, suh; that's a fairly close tally too. Five brands all under a trail brand. We'll form the leaders and move out day after tomorrow." He paused to look at the herd. "By my own figures, I calculate at no time will that herd ever completely stop movin' north."

"I don't believe I understand," Heinz said.

"Why, it's simple when you think about it, suh. With so large a herd on the trail, the point will move at dawn, and it will be dark before the drag commences to move. A magnificent sight, suh. Stirs the heart, it surely does."

"It's going to stir the heart if those cattle ever stampede," Heinz said. "Think on that."

General Pritchard's usually gray manner turned sunny. "Why, I expect 'em to. Many times. It's all in the business. All in the business." Then he wheeled about and Heinz rode on in to the main house with them, thinking how good a bath and a change of clothes would be.

7

Great preparations were being made at the Pritchard place to celebrate the commencement of the cattle drive and families came from miles around and three huge pits had been dug and filled with hot coals and beef wrapped tightly in soaked sacks was buried there to cook a day and a night. General Pritchard sent a message to Colonel Shannon and select officers of his command to attend this function, but Captain Paul Dane was pointedly omitted.

It was, Heinz thought, the biggest party he had ever seen; he estimated that four hundred people gathered in the yard, and a gay affair it was, in spite of the fact that these Texans were class conscious. The land owners were congregated around the house, while the paid hands stayed in the yard. It was not that these people did not get along or stayed to themselves; they mingled freely, but the paid hands knew their place and stayed there.

Pritchard did some private entertaining in his library; Mitchell Shannon was there, and Carl Heinz, and Race Daniels. The whiskey was good and everyone was in a fair humor, particularly Nathan Pritchard who stood on the threshold of being a rich man, or one completely ruined.

"I would like to propose a toast," he said. "To the railroad a thousand miles away; may we reach it safely."

They drank to that, then Shannon said, "General, you're going to run into Indians and outlaws and weather. It's a big risk."

"Suh, all my life I've taken big risks. This does not deter me."

"Commendable spirit," Shannon said. He crossed his legs and held his whiskey glass delicately balanced on his knee. "Once a herd gets through, the trail will belong to anyone. And people travel two ways on a trail, general. They come in wagons with their plows and life's savings and there'll be no way to stop them. The big speculator hasn't hit this part of Texas yet because all they see is open range and cattle a thousand miles from the nearest market. But if you show them how to get those cattle to market, they'll swarm into this country and buy up everything they can get their hands on."

"I know that," Pritchard said. "That's why it's important for Texas men to get there, sell a few herd, and have some ammunition money." He shook his finger at Shannon. "We may have lost the war, suh, but I'll be damned if we lose Texas."

"I wouldn't want you to forget, general, that you're under the authority of a military government," Shannon said. "And one of our functions is to restore peace and order."

"But not prosperity," Heinz said. "Colonel, a man needs more than peace and order. He needs a job with a regular thirty dollars a month and found. I know, sir, that it is the opinion of certain political leaders that this money has to come from the north. That's true, but the rub comes in how it gets to Texas. By legitimate trade? Or in the pockets of opportunists and speculators?"

"These things do adjust themselves in time," Shannon said.

"Yes, but I agree with the general, sir. Texas lost the war but she doesn't want to lose Texas."

"Captain Dane came to me, storming about the issuing of firearms," Shannon said. "Carl, I know you acted within the letter of the law, but—"

"Then what is there to say about it, suh?" Nathan Pritchard asked. "Don't your Yankee politicians realize they will never disarm Texas? Your troops could search us every day and we'd still hide our guns. Why, how would we defend ourselves against the Indians?"

Mitchell Shannon smiled. "From the story I get, your men did pretty well a week ago. Dane's talking about confiscating your horses; he has the right, you know."

"Then why isn't he here trying it?" Heinz asked.

"Because I've sent him south of Marfa to look for a dangerous killer called Hardin," Shannon said. "Carl, I'm not out of sympathy with what you're trying to do. Unofficially, I hope you carry it off. Officially, I'd prefer not to know anything about it." He had a refill of his whiskey glass. "Most of the politicians in Washington have never been to Texas and do not intend to come here. They believe that every man here is a potential insurrectionist, ready to resume hostilities against the Union at the slightest provocation. Hence, I'm supposed to establish a firm military government. Captain Dane's police are supposed to keep order in this area." He shrugged. "Carl Heinz believes this is the wrong way. Unofficially, I might agree with him. But I'm a professional soldier, and general, you're the last man who would forgive me for not following orders, right or wrong." His glance touched Heinz. "I gave you the rifles and ammunition. It was all I could do. You under-stand that."

"Yes, I do," Heinz said. "Dane wants to change the law in relation to owning or possessing firearms."

"He'll have difficulty there," Shannon said softly. "And that's all I'm going to say on the matter."

"There is a change in your manner, suh," Race Daniels said. "Oh, you were cordial enough at our last meeting, but now I detect a new sincerity—"

"You might thank Mr. Heinz for that," Shannon said. "Let me tell you about Mr. Heinz, gentle-men, for I'm sure he hasn't told you this himself. During his studies at the Academy, he established an academic standard never before achieved. Mr. Heinz is not a tactical commander and has never pretended to be. His specialty is planning, logistics, and having been his commanding officer for three years, I can truth-fully say that he could teach most generals a thing or two. Mr. Heinz is also an idealist. Were he a civilian he would be a scholar or philosopher. But he was a professional soldier who gave up his career over a point of policy. That wasn't an easy thing to do, and because he did it, I did some thinking of my own and as a consequence, overhauled some of my fundamental policies. The main one being to carefully with-draw, a bit at a time, the authority of these so called state police." He looked at each of them. "However, if that ever got out of this room, I'd have to run the risk of calling you liars."

Pritchard laughed. "If I ever repeated it, suh, I'd be a liar." He got up and the meeting ended and they went outside, but Shannon stayed close to Carl Heinz and they stood on the porch and watched the festivities.

Shannon said, "Some day you may be a state legislator, or the governor."

Heinz laughed. "Colonel, I like Texas. I think it's a good place to live. That's all there is to it, no ulterior motives, no ax to grind." He heard a light step behind him and found Cecilia Pritchard standing in the doorway.

"I heard that," she said and came forward. "Mr. Heinz, can you understand why it was hard for me to trust you?"

"Yes." He smiled and offered his hand. "Friends now?"

"Very good friends," she said and held his hand. "Colonel, you're missing some very fine barbeque."

"Indeed I must be," Shannon said and bowed and walked away.

"Now I wish I could dismiss superior officers like that," Heinz said. "But of course it takes wavy brown hair and big blue eyes."

"I wanted to talk to you alone," Cecilia said. "Shall we go inside?" She took his arm and they went into the drawing room and closed the door and the sounds of the laughter and dancing were shut out a bit. "I want to ask you a question and I'd like a straight answer."

"If I can give it," he said.

"You told father you'd borrow money from the officers on the post, but you didn't, did you?"

"No, it was my money," he admitted.

"Why didn't you tell him that?"

He shrugged. "Mainly because I owe him nothing and he knows that. By—well, the way I did it, I introduced the profit motive and he could understand that."

"Those people out there, laughing and dancing and having a good time," Cecilia said, "is something that just hasn't happened for over three years. The future has some hope for them. Tomorrow is not going to be as bleak as yesterday. Some of them will be gone for almost a year. Some might not come back, but that's only danger and they can live with that. It's the hope they have now that's important. And Carl, if the cattle don't get to market, they'll have been better because of this hope."

"They'll make it to the railhead," Heinz said.

"I think so too, but do you see my point?"

"Yes."

She came up to him and put her hands on his shoulders, then raised on her tiptoes and kissed him. He was surprised and pleased and put his arms around her and the door opened quickly and Nan said, "Cec—oh, I'm terribly sorry. I really am."

She closed the door and Heinz and Cecilia stepped apart. "Damn," she said. "She'll misunderstand that."

"Is it that important?" Heinz asked.

She looked at him oddly for a moment, then said, "I'll do what I can."

After she went out, he lighted a cigar and stood there a moment, puffing gently, then he left the house by the side entrance and walked around the yard until he found Ed Leslie and his brother. Ed had his arm in a sling but he seemed to be in no pain and then Heinz saw the shine in his eyes and knew why.

"You'd better be sober enough to ride tomorrow," Heinz said jokingly.

"No matter how much I drink," Ed said, "I'm always cold sober the next day. But Joe gets sick. He can't take the booze. A quart and he's about had it."

"Sure to hell wish you was goin' with us," Joe Leslie said. "I kinda took a likin' to you."

"My job is here," Heinz said. "Every man to what he does best." He kept looking around, watching the crowd, and this drew Ed Leslie's attention.

"You keep watchin', Carl. Expectin' somebody?"

"In a way," Heinz said. "I'll see you later."

He moved around for almost an hour, then he saw a buggy coming toward the ranch and went out to meet it. Captain Paul Dane got down and whipped dust from his uniform.

"I heard there was a soiree going on out here," Dane said. "Thought I'd investigate it."

"Why don't I save you the trouble?" Heinz asked. "This is a private party, invitations only. You weren't invited."

"You've had it in for me—"

"That's putting it mildly," Heinz said, cutting him off. The two Leslie boys came up and he said, "Take the captain's horse and rig to the barn."

Joe said, "He ain't stayin', is he?"

"The captain and I are going to have a private talk," Heinz said. "One that's been long overdue." He took Dane by the arm and when he tried to jerk away, Heinz tightened his grip and ripped the captain's sleeve slightly.

"You clumsy jackass—"

"Shut your mouth!" Heinz said and led Dane around the crowd and to the barn without attracting any attention at all, or at least not from anyone who cared to come over and see what was going on.

Dane walked a good twenty yards before he balked, and Heinz stopped and said, "How long has it been since you've been mauled in the dirt?"

"What?"

"Now you walk on ahead or I'll maul you right here and now, in front of all these people," Heinz declared. "What'll it be?"

"Have your way," Dane said and walked on. "But you can't get away with anything."

Joe Leslie had the barn door open and he closed it when they stepped inside. Heinz gave Dane a shove, then leaned against the door. "I thought you were sent to Marfa to find Hardin?"

"He's not in Marfa," Dane said. "What's it to you anyway?"

"How bad do you want him?" Heinz asked.

"When I find him, I'll show you," Dane said and patted his pistol holster.

Heinz smiled and said, "Joe, where's Hardin?"

"The last time I saw him he was feedin' his face," Joe said.

"You go ask him to step in here," Heinz said.

Dane's eyes got round. "What do you think you're going to do, Heinz?"

"Why, I'm not just too sure, but I'm going to give you a chance to show all those people out there the calibre of man they have keeping law and order. I'm going to let you take Hardin into custody while they're all watching."

"The man's a killer," Dane said. "Did you ever see the way he carries his pistol? He's got the flap cut off the holster and—" He fell silent for a moment. "I see what you're doing. You're trying to get me killed."

Heinz said, "Stay with him, Ed."

"Why sure." He leaned against the door when Heinz stepped outside and saw Wes Hardin coming across the yard with Joe Leslie.

He stopped Hardin twenty yards from the barn and said, "Let me have your gun."

"Wait now, I don't give up my gun easy."

78

"Neither do I," Heinz said. "But I did once and I didn't argue about it."

"So you did," Hardin said and handed the Navy Colt over.

Heinz knocked out the barrel wedge, took out the cylinder and pried off the percussion caps, then reassembled the gun and jammed it back into Hardin's holster.

"It won't shoot that way," Hardin said curiously.

"No, but you might scare a man half to death with it." He turned to Joe Leslie. "All right, bring Captain Dane out here and let him make his arrest."

He looked at the crowd and saw that many were watching and he felt a little sorry for Dane, sorry that he had to be the one to go on his knees, but Heinz could see no other way of breaking the police power other than shooting, and he didn't want that.

8

Colonel Mitchell Shannon saw what was coming off and he came forward quickly and said, "Heinz, don't do this. Dane hasn't got a chance and you know it. Hardin, if you kill this man—"

"Hardin won't kill him," Heinz said quickly, then Dane came out of the barn and stood there; Joe Leslie had to push him a little to get room to close the door. Then he and Ed stepped out of the line of fire.

"I hear you've been lookin' for me," Hardin said. He stood there, loose and gangly and dangerous and it was frightening to watch him, a machine with no particular conscience. He kept waiting for Dane to move, and finally he said, "Well, go ahead and arrest me."

"I—I arrest you," Dane said.

"Ain't you goin' to take my gun?" Hardin invited.

"This has gone—" Shannon started to say, but stopped when Carl Heinz shook his head. Then he spoke to Dane in a softer tone, one filled with sympathy. "Go on back to your post, captain. Go on now before—" He shook his head. "Just get out of here."

"That man is in my custody," Dane said, his expression frozen.

"Is he really?" Shannon said. "Dane, you're the only one who can lose here. Get out."

"Why the hell don't you back me?" Dane shouted. "I'll write a report on this!" He flung his arms wide and hurried to his buggy and drove away, lashing the team furiously.

Wes Hardin said, "Can I put caps back on my pistol now, Mister Heinz?"

He laughed and wheeled and walked away and Shannon blew out a long breath. "So you had it rigged all the time? If Dane had come up to it—"

"I didn't think he would," Heinz said. He looked

80

searchingly at Shannon. "You could have helped him but you didn't."

"I think you knew I wouldn't," Shannon said. "All my military life I've taken pride in treating justly the men I actively disliked, but this time I just couldn't do it. Heinz, you cut the legs out from that man; people are going to talk about this and hereafter it's going to be harder for him to make his rules stick. To be effective, Dane has to have some people with him, some informers, some favorseekers. He would have been better off if he'd called Hardin's bluff." He turned his head and looked toward the table where the beef was being cut. "I heard he killed a Texan. Doesn't anyone here care?"

"Not enough to take it up with him," Carl Heinz said. "Colonel, I'm not passing judgment on these people, and I don't want them to pass it on me. Some of us have been trying to go by the old rules and I don't think they apply anymore. Do you know what I mean?"

"Yes," Shannon said. "There is something about this country that brings out the weaknesses in a man, and some of my own I don't like." He reached out and tapped Heinz on the chest. "If you have any more ideas up your sleeve, save them until after I leave."

Heinz saw Nan Pritchard sitting alone on the west porch and he got a plate of meat and beans and walked over as though he had accidentally strayed in that direction. He stood before a vacant chair and said, "Is this reserved for some nice young man?"

"Are you a nice young man?"

"By my own standards," Heinz said and sat down.

"You and Cecilia have reached an understanding, I see," Nan said.

"Well, she got around to trusting me, if that's what you mean."

"It's not what I mean and you know it."

"The kiss wasn't what it looked like," he said.

"It looked like what it was," she said. "Mr. Heinz—"

"You were calling me Carl."

"In this frame of mind I'll call you Mr. Heinz."

"I see," he said. "Excuse the interruption."

"When two people of the opposite sex put their lips together, that's a kiss, isn't it?"

"Yes," he said, "that's a good definition."

"That's what I saw, you and Cecilia kissing," she said. "I'm assuming that it wasn't done lightly."

"If you mean the pressure—"

She stamped her foot. "You know damned well what I meant!"

"Oh," he said, "did you realize that you swore?"

She started to get up and he quickly put down his plate and took her arms and held her from leaving. Then he said, "I wonder if you're angry because it was Cecilia I kissed and not you?"

"If you kiss me," she said, "I'll slap your face."

"That hardly seems too much to pay," he said and pulled her to him and kissed her hard and when he released her she gasped and slapped him. She thought it was over, but it wasn't; he kissed her again and she slapped him again and he kissed her three more times and she slapped him only twice.

"You missed one," he said.

"Your cheek's red," she said. "Doesn't it hurt?"

"What is pain compared to the delight of your lips?"

"Oh, can't you be serious?" She tried to pull away but he still held her.

"Serious? I couldn't be more," Heinz said. "But I didn't think you wanted me to rush things."

She smiled brightly. "You've misjudged me. Rush things."

"Here? Now?"

"Well, you've been standing here in broad daylight in full view of several hundred people and kissing me so this is hardly the time to get sneaky about it."

He turned his head and looked and found a lot of people smiling and watching him, and his face got very red. "Talk about a jackass," he said and shook his head.

Nan smiled and patted his hand. "We have a saying here, that we're 'declared.' That means you've made your intentions clear in public and no man would think of stepping between us now."

"What have I declared?" Heinz asked. "Or do I have to guess?"

"Papa will want a big wedding," Nan said. She looked at him and kept smiling and he couldn't make up his mind whether he'd been pulled into this or walked with his eyes open. "That day in town, I took a shine to you right off," she said. "Couldn't you tell?"

"Honestly, no," Heinz said. "Look, do we have to stand out here with everyone looking?"

"We can go inside," she said. "Did you want to kiss me again?"

"You ought to be spanked," he said, and saw General Pritchard walking toward the porch. "I suppose he wants to shake my hand?"

"Naturally," Nan said and moved on to the side entrance.

The sight of the herd moving was, Heinz believed, something he would never forget if he lived to be eighty. The chuck wagons and horse wranglers had moved out a little after midnight and they would go on ahead ten miles, select a camp site and be ready when the first of the herd reached them. Two more wagons went with the herd for there were so many animals strung out so far that there would always be two camps, one making up and one moving.

All that day cattle passed in view and by

nightfall the dust was still thick in the air and the people who had come from miles around to watch this went home. General Pritchard's two sons were in command of the herd, and supper that evening seemed rather bare with them gone.

They had their coffee brought to the general's study and he said, "Tomorrow I think we can start for Windridge's place. It's eighty miles to the northeast, near the Indian country. Talked to some folks here who mentioned that Windridge was trying to put together a herd."

"Do you know him?"

"Occasional acquaintance," Pritchard said. "He'll listen to me, if that's what you mean. Have you the funds to finance another drive?"

"Yes," Heinz said. "It won't be as easy as the first though."

Pritchard arched an eyebrow. "I had it in mind that it would be easier."

"It would be if we'd already got a herd through," Heinz said. "Windridge may not want to go so far on faith."

"God, man, there seems little else left but faith," Pritchard said. "Well, I was never a man to go into battle with a short supply of ammunition. What do you suggest?"

"I wish I was in a position to buy his herd if he wouldn't risk it alone," Heinz said. "Do you know how many head he has?"

"He runs big," Pritchard said, doing some

mental figuring. "Over a thousand head. Maybe two. It's hard to say with stock breeding wild."

"If a man could pay five a head," Heinz said, "and take the risks of driving, he could come out with a hundred per cent profit."

"More, if he knew the trails," Pritchard said. He squinted his eyes. "Are you thinking what I'm thinking?" Then he slapped his leg and laughed. "But where do we get the money?"

"I've got two thousand," Heinz said. "Who's getting most of the soldier and police money?"

"Pete Burgess in Marfa," Pritchard said. "He owns the saloon there and in town." He stopped for a moment. "It might pay to ride over there first and have a talk."

"That's Dane's stronghold," Heinz said. "Some risk."

Pritchard laughed. "Suh, if that man or any of his police approached me, I'll put a ball between their eyes." He brought out a pair of his excellent cigars. "Pete is a man known to be tight. I don't hold much chance of breakin' him loose from a gold piece."

"But you think it's worth a try?"

"When there's nothin' else to do, a charge is always worth a try," Pritchard said.

They left early with two saddle horses and a pack horse and arrived in Marfa late in the afternoon and tied up before the hotel and took a room there; afterward they went to the saloon, ordered a drink, and waited for Pete Burgess to come on his evening shift.

He checked the till carefully, then noticed Carl Heinz and after a moment he came down the bar and said, "Say, ain't you the—"

"Yes," Heinz said. "I got my gun back. Wes has yours."

Burgess grinned and wiped the bar. "Good. The boy's due to be hung, but I knew his pappy." Then he looked at Nathan Pritchard and shook hands. "Didn't hardly recognize you out of uniform, general. I'd offer you one on the house, but things have been kind of tight." He rolled his eyes at four Negro police sitting at one table, splitting one bottle. "Only the wrong kind of people have money. A man can't even enjoy his own prejudices without starving."

"Could we talk some business?" Heinz asked.

"Sure, come on in the back room." He spoke to the day man. "Stick around awhile longer, Harry." Then he led the way, saw that they had chairs, and crossed his arms. "What's on your mind?"

"Pete, how would you like to go in the cattle business?"

Burgess shook his head. "Not for me."

"The general just started a herd north to market," Heinz said.

"Heard that," Burgess said. "Never been done before, has it?"

"No," Pritchard said, "but we'll do it."

"How do you know there's a market there?" Burgess asked.

"I saw the town and the railroad, and the cattle buyers," Heinz said. "Pete, I've got two thousand in gold."

"That's a lot of money."

"But I need more."

"I'm a poor man."

Heinz smiled. "You're making your share. The only ready cash in Texas is the police and army payroll and they slip most of it over your bar."

"Business ain't what it used to be."

"It could come back," Pritchard said. "But we have to help it along."

"When those drovers get back from Kansas," Heinz said, "they'll have money in their pockets. Only there's got to be more. The general and I want to buy cattle and start another herd north. Then another."

Burgess shook his head. "Big risks."

"So's sitting here taking it in a dime at a time," Heinz said.

"Still a big risk," Burgess said.

"The night I helped out your friend, the risks were big. I could have had my neck stretched if I'd been caught."

"I don't see what that's—"

"You're for Texas, aren't you?"

"Yes, but—"

88

"Then you can't sit here and hope things will get better. You've got to make them better."

"But I don't think I ought—"

"Pete, all I have in the world is two thousand in gold," Heinz said. "This isn't my fight, but I'm willing to put that money on the block."

"Well, I need operating capital."

"I'm not asking for all of it."

"How much then?" Burgess said.

"Five thousand."

"Five thousand?" He quieted down. "Why, that's—"

"That's a drop in the bucket to what you can make," Heinz said. "It's a three way split, Pete. Isn't that right, general?"

"I was thinking more of twenty-five per cent," he said.

"Well, yes. I got a little carried away," Heinz said. "What about it, Pete? Hesitate now and you may pass up something you'll be sorry for the rest of your life. Look, in that barn, I didn't hesitate. I acted and Hardin's alive and kicking. Now you're in the same spot. You've got a chance to be one of the biggest men in Texas. As big as the general, maybe."

"When do you need the money?" Burgess asked.

"How soon can you get it?" Pritchard asked.

"Today, if there's a rush."

"We don't want to lose time," Pritchard said.

"Bring it to the hotel room and I'll have papers made out."

"I guess I can do business your way," Burgess said. "With a handshake." He looked intently at Heinz. "Man, you can sure be persuasive. I hope I don't regret this—"

9

General Pritchard liked to live high even when he couldn't afford it; he had a bottle sent to his room and he and Carl Heinz sat by the window and looked down at the street and drank good whiskey.

Finally Pritchard said, "I've known Pete Burgess casually for many years and I never thought he'd be persuaded to part with his cash." He turned his head and looked at Heinz. "You've seen the man once, yet you felt sure. Would you tell me why, suh?"

"Because I don't think Burgess really likes the saloon business," Heinz said. "He hates the police and he has no use for the army, and they're his only real cash customers. I had the notion that maybe he'd like to branch out. He could make a lot of money, general."

"The day will come quicker than we think when we'll need a lot of money," Pritchard said. He heard a firm step in the hall and got up and opened the door. Pete Burgess took off his hat and stepped inside, his manner hesitant.

"Do you want to back out?" Heinz asked.

"I'm not a man to go back on my word," Burgess said. He took a sack from beneath his shirt and handed it to Nathan Pritchard. "You'll find it's all there. I counted it three times."

Pritchard wrote out a receipt and signed it and handed it to Burgess. The man hesitated and Pritchard thrust it into his shirt pocket, saying, "We're going to be handling a lot of cattle and money and I want this done legal and proper. I'll see that you get a copy of the agreement to sign."

"Anything you say, general. Your word's good enough for me."

"That may be all right between us," Pritchard said, "but if I died, you'd have a hard time getting your money back. It's all business, you understand. You keep books, don't you?"

"No, I don't," Burgess said. "I just take the money in, pay my bills, and pocket the difference." He grinned. "And I've got honest bartenders." He clapped his hat on his head. "Well, I've got to get back." He turned to the door and opened it, then stood there looking at the sack of money. "I sure hope I ain't been talked into nothin'."

After he went down the stairs, Pritchard said, "There's a man with doubts, Carl."

"He has no more than I have," Heinz said. "Burgess worries about losing his shirt, but I

91

know there's a lot more to be lost." He took off his boots and stretched out on the bed. "You do what you want, general. I'm going to get some sleep."

In the three months that followed, Carl Heinz knew no permanent home; he was either riding or attending to the office they had opened in Marfa. Many of his nights were spent on the prairie, or at some rancher's house. People he had never seen before knew him on sight, and he bought cattle, had them gathered, and on a blistering summer day another herd moved north, six thousand head, and after they were moving he realized how much of a job it had been to get them on their way. That herd was the product of a lot of dickering, and according to the books he had paid an average of five dollars and eighteen cents a head, a total of thirty-one thousand and two hundred dollars.

Not all in cash; he had paid half in cash, the balance after the herd was sold in Abilene. The money? He'd picked up a few gray hairs over that for he had hardly gotten started when he realized that he was running out of cash. But somehow he had an equity, one he hadn't counted on, and that was the first herd moving north. One of the riders had broken a leg and he came back with a second cousin and the report went through the country like a brush fire: the Pritchard boys were driving hard, averaging thirteen to fifteen miles a day and when the two men left, the herd was only a day south of the Canadian. They fought off two Indian attacks and one stampede which took no lives, and the news was almost as good as a rebel victory two years before.

Some of the men who had sold Carl Heinz cattle came to him with money in hand, wanting to put some of it back in this company. After talking to Pritchard and Burgess, they agreed to hold half the assets and sell shares. Colonel Mitchell Shannon surprised Heinz by offering a loan against the profit Heinz stood to make off the first herd, and the Texas Cattle Company had nine thousand dollars in the bank, six thousand head of cattle on the trail, and the prospects for bigger drives in the spring. And Heinz, who was clever with a pencil, figured their assets to be in the neighborhood of a hundred and seventy thousand Yankee dollars come spring.

If they didn't lose a herd.

The prospect of making money was a honeypot that would attract some sharp bees and Heinz knew it and waited for it and he didn't have to wait long. Captain Dane and a squad of police rode into town in the middle of a sweltering afternoon, escorting a well-dressed man driving a buggy, and by the evening meal, Carl Heinz knew that Caleb Early was going to buy cattle and pay cash on the barrel head.

The man took a suite at the hotel, three rooms, and had a carpenter come in and remodel the place and he paid cash for that, which stirred up some talk. Heinz got it from Pete Burgess, who eventually heard everything, that Caleb Early was some shirt-tail kin to Paul Dane.

The Texas Cattle Company's office was a small cubicle that had once housed a boot maker, long gone out of business, and the furniture was whatever Heinz could gather up. He knew it wasn't much for looks, but it was solid, and it was Texas owned, which he figured would be the tipping factor in the long pull.

Heinz made no attempt to meet Caleb Early; he figured Early would make the first call, and he did. He was a tall, handsome man, always well-dressed, and the heat didn't seem to bother him at all while it made Heinz sweat and smell and constantly dirtied clean collars.

Early whipped some dust off a chair with his gloves and sat down. "Allow me to introduce myself," Early said.

"I know who you are and you know who I am," Heinz said. "Why spar?"

"I agree," he said, smiling. "It's much too hot for that." He crossed his long legs and his coat fell apart a bit and Heinz saw the butt of a pearl-handled pistol in some kind of a shoulder holster. "We're competitors, it seems."

"Well, you have the idea anyway," Heinz said. "But you have to buy and drive and sell and get back with the profit. And you'll have to wait until next spring. Put a herd north now and they'll hit Kansas in the dead of winter. Pretty rough going, if they could get through at all."

Early smiled and waved his hand. "You have the jump on me there, Mr. Heinz, but I think it'll be different in the spring." He waved his hand at the poorly appointed office. "You're operating on a shoe-string and everyone knows it. Wait until you start buying."

"Going to up the price a little?"

Early took a cigar from his case and put a match to it. "I can double your price and not raise a sweat."

Carl Heinz thought about that, then said, "Not without a tie in at the railhead." Then he leaned back and nodded. "I see. Drawing fat from both ends of the hog. That's good, if you can get away with it."

"I intend to," Caleb Early said. "I'd also like to make you an offer for your business."

"You'd be wasting your time," Heinz said. "It isn't for sale."

Early laughed. "Mr. Heinz, *everything's* for sale if the price is right. Twenty thousand?"

"That's a joke and you know it."

Caleb Early shook his head. "Do I look like a disorganized man? Believe me, I'm not joking. There'll be a time when you'll beg me to offer twenty thousand." He uncrossed his legs and stood up. "You have a dark look on your face, like a man harboring violent thoughts. Good day, sir. We'll talk again."

He left and Heinz sat for a moment, then threw his pencil across the room. Quite easily he could dismiss this as arrogance, a big bluff, but he knew better; Caleb Early wasn't bluffing. No, he had his hand backed with some high cards that he hadn't even played yet.

Carl Heinz didn't like to admit to worrying, but he wished that some word would come through about the Pritchard herd. If he only knew where they were, or whether they'd gotten to Abilene— but he didn't know. All he had to go on was hope and damned little money.

Once a week he rode to the Pritchard ranch to see Nan and he usually stayed two days; he heard more news there than he did in town because Pritchard's skeleton crew got around and talked and brought it all back to the main house.

The general was not openly concerned, but Heinz noticed that he was quieter, given to spending more hours alone in the library or study and Heinz knew that he was worried about his sons and the rest of the men and all those cattle; it was a grave responsibility for one man to have, and if it didn't come off, if the herd did not reach Abilene, Pritchard would be blamed.

When Heinz was alone with Nan, she spoke of it, but went about it in a woman's way, through another subject. They were sitting before the fireplace for there was a chill in the air and the huge house was never easy to heat.

"Carl, why would Caleb Early want to buy cattle now?" she asked.

He took the cigar from his mouth and looked at her. "I didn't know that he was."

"He tried to buy Fred Slade's herd."

"I don't know him. Where's his place?"

"About twenty-five miles to the south. Father wanted him to join the first drive, but he wouldn't take the chance. Some of our men drop in on him now and then; he's pretty isolated, he and his family. Slade said that Early had been out there but he'd turned him down."

Carl Heinz frowned. "That sounds odd. A man would be a fool to buy now, feed all winter, then drive in the spring. He'd have to rent land and hire riders." He shook his head. "There must be some mistake."

"Maybe you ought to talk to him, Carl?"

Heinz shrugged. "It might not hurt. In the spring we'll want to buy his herd and it wouldn't be good business to have him think Early was the only one interested enough to see him." He looked at her. "Do you suppose one of the hands could show me—"

"Why, I thought I'd do that," Nan said.

He showed his surprise. "That would be a two day—I mean, do you think your father would consider it proper if we were alone—"

She laughed softly. "Carl, we can't help it because people live far apart. We have an honor system out here when we travel. It's kind of like bundling used to be, only on the move."

"I see," he said. "I didn't mean to sound like a prude or anything, but I was thinking—"

"Stop thinking," she said. "We can leave in the morning and arrive at Slade's tomorrow night. Father will feel better about it if he knows the truth."

"Why would he worry about Slade?"

"Because he's a Texan, and a neighbor," Nan said. "When he came here, this was open range, and he built this whole empire, worked twenty years to do it. Any law we had was what my father made and enforced. He has a responsibility, Carl. As long as he lives he'll have it. Some would think it foolish, this Pritchard honor, but sometimes it's all he's had to go on."

"Texans aren't the only ones who have it," Heinz said. Then he reached for her hand. "Would you care for a glass of wine before we say goodnight?"

"Yes. Here, before the fire." She got up and yanked on the bell cord to summon the servant.

They left early, with two saddle horses and a pack horse and pushed south across dry rolling land. A wind from the northeast promised some raw weather and the sky was leaden, overcast, with thick roiling clouds.

He had planned a noon stop, to make some coffee at least, but even their slickers did not keep out the cold and he decided to keep moving. He kept watching the sky and measuring the whip of the wind and couldn't make up his mind whether it would rain or snow; it was at that time of the year when either was possible.

In the late afternoon the sky let go and it came down in wet, melting flakes that made travel even more miserable. It soaked the saddles and their jeans and ran down their collars and he had half a mind to pitch a shelter and spend the night on the prairie. But he thought of Nan sleeping in a tarp on the ground and decided it would be best to make Slade's place and get her in bed, with a warm fire.

Maintaining a direction was difficult, with the horizon a smudge and the sky cut off by the clouds, but his army training kept him moving southward and Nan recognized several creeks and finally they could see Slade's place backed against a wooded draw, a cabin sheltered by trees.

A dog came running out to greet them, barking and running under the horses' feet and they tied up by the corral. The place seemed deserted, and this struck Heinz as odd, and he said, "Wait here," and walked on to the cabin.

When he rounded the corner he saw Fred Slade face down in the yard, his rifle by him, and when Heinz bent and touched him he knew from the coldness, the stiffness, that Slade had been dead many hours.

The woman was inside, slumped against the wall, and Slade's oldest boy, a lad of fourteen, was sprawled by the door. Heinz stepped outside and met Nan coming toward the cabin; he stopped her and said, "They're all dead."

Her mouth went round. "No! How could they be?"

"Go on in the barn," he said gently. "Go on now. I'll bury them and call you when it's done."

"Carl, I'm not so weak—"

"Oh, I know that," he said. "But why should you have to see it and remember it? Go on now. It shouldn't take me more than an hour."

10

Full darkness fell before Carl Heinz finished burying the Slade family, and as he worked alone, he drew some conclusions based on what his eyes saw. Slade had not been surprised by anyone; he had come out of his cabin unarmed; Heinz could tell because Slade had been shot in the back, probably as he ran to the door to get his gun, and there was a trail of blood leading there, and one leading back to the place where he had died. Afterward, the attackers had fought their way into the house, killed the woman and the boy, then ridden away. He figured six, from the tracks in the yard, and at least one of them had been wounded for he found splotches of blood on the ground.

After the burying, he straightened the cabin, threw some rugs over the spots on the floor where blood had soaked into the wood and then went to the barn to get Nan.

She was shivering with cold; her clothes were wet and moisture squished in her boots when she walked and he hurriedly built up a fire while she took off her clothes, then standing in her bloomers and shirtwaist, backed close to the heat to steam dry.

Heinz made a point not to look at her while he mixed the pancake batter and sliced bacon he'd found in the back room, but he thought it strange, their being alone this way; it would have never happened to an Eastern girl; she would have died of the cough before taking off her clothes in front of a man.

After they had eaten he stripped to his woolen underwear and they hung their clothes on the backs of chairs and put a blanket on the floor so they could sit with their backs against the wall and their feet toward the fire. Heinz let the fire in the iron cook stove go out and let the fireplace heat the room and that was the only light they had.

Finally he said, "I put it around breakfast time. The sink was full of washed dishes. Mrs. Slade was at the sink when the first shot was fired. The boy was in the pantry; there is an armload of firewood scattered on the floor where he dropped it and rushed for his gun." He pointed to a corner near a bedroom door. "He fell there, shot just as he came out. But his rifle was empty so he got off a shot. Hit something too because by the entrance door there's some specks of blood, waist high, on the door frame."

"Could it have been Indians?"

Heinz shook his head. "The horses were still in the barn. What Indian would pass up horses?" He thought a moment. "Not Mexicans either. Nothing's taken. Slade had two ten dollar gold pieces in his pocket."

"Then they were just—murdered?" Nan asked. "Who would do that?"

"I don't know, or why," Heinz said. He got up and found his pants dry enough to put on, and he tossed Nan's jeans to her. "We'll get out of here first thing in the morning. I think Colonel Shannon ought to know of this."

He spread some more blankets and banked the fire and settled down beside her. "Your father ought to send a crew and round up Slade's herd. He has relatives, hasn't he?"

"I wouldn't know of any." She pulled the scratchy blanket to her chin and rested her head on her arm. "What are you thinking of, Carl?"

"Finding that wounded man," Heinz said. "Now go to sleep."

She smiled. "No kiss?"

"I've been looking at your bare legs for an hour;

I don't want to start anything." He rolled over, tucked his blanket around him, and went to sleep.

Twice during the night the cold woke him and he got up to stoke the fire, and just before dawn he got up again and made a fire in the cook stove. He made some pan biscuits, heated some beans he found in a crock, and cooked some side meat, and they were eating this when he heard horsemen approaching. Heinz quickly left the table, picked up his Henry repeater and opened the door a crack, just enough to see and to point the gun.

Captain Paul Dane rode in with four men and when he saw Heinz he drew up and said, "What's going on here? Where's Slade?"

Heinz stepped outside and pointed to the graves he'd dug under the trees. Dane said, "His family too?"

"All three."

He dismounted. "Who did it?"

"He was dead when we got here," Heinz said.

Dane looked up sharply. "We?"

"Nan Pritchard's inside," Heinz said.

Dane smiled. "My, that's cozy, isn't it?"

"Watch your mouth," Heinz said.

"No offense meant." He took off his heavy gloves and blew on his hands. "You don't know anything about this?"

"Not a thing."

Dane nodded, then said, "You could have done this."

"I didn't though. Think of something else."

"Now I have just your word for that," Dane said. "Heinz, you may be in trouble."

"I don't think so," Heinz said. "It's one jump back for me and I'm inside with this repeater and a lot of ammunition. Do you think you'd like to come in after me?"

"If you fire on us," Dane said, "you'll never stop running."

"I'm not going to fire on you," Heinz told him, "because you're too smart to make a stupid accusation and hope it'll stick. Isn't that right, captain?"

"Yes," Dane said. "I'm not backing down from you, just doing what I think is best."

"What are you doing here?"

"Routine patrol," Dane said. "Have you got that good a reason?"

"Nan wanted to visit," Heinz said. "That's not against any new law, is it?"

"No," Dane said and got on his horse. He wheeled and led his detail out of the yard and when they pulled from sight Carl Heinz stood there his brows knotted. Nan came out and looked curiously at him.

"That's a funny look on your face," she said.

"I just thought of something," Heinz said. "That fat sergeant of Dane's wasn't with him today."

"Is that important?"

"I've never seen Dane without him," Heinz

104

said. "He's kind of a black hand-maiden. Anyway, I'm going to ask where he was."

He went inside and rolled their blankets, carried them to the barn and loaded the pack horse. Ten minutes later they started north.

Snow was still falling, lightly, and the temperature had dropped just enough to hold it, and even though it was colder, riding was more comfortable because they weren't wet.

They saw no one on the prairie and toward nightfall they raised the Pritchard ranch and Nan went on into the house while Carl Heinz put up the horses. As he started toward the house, the general came out and met him.

"Nan told me about Slade. A terrible thing. I'll have some men make a night ride of it. They can be on the property by morning." He walked back to the house with Heinz. "I think you should make a full report of this to Colonel Shannon."

"I intend to," Heinz said. "But I'd like to write it and have one of your men deliver it. I want to go to Marfa and ask a few questions. Slade or his boy hit one of the men who attacked him. That man has to go somewhere, general."

"I see your point," Pritchard said. "Use caution now."

"My intention exactly," Heinz said.

Although he was tired, Heinz had a fresh horse saddled and made a night ride to Marfa, arriving very late. He pulled up in front of the saloon and tied his horse and went in because he was cold and hungry and he knew Pete Burgess had a good free lunch counter.

Burgess nodded as Heinz came up to the bar and ordered a whiskey, then a glass of beer; the whiskey was to put a little fire in him while the beer was to enjoy.

Business was thin. Three Negro police stood at the far end, talking softly and after Heinz made himself a sandwich, he took his beer and idled down that way.

"Can I buy you a drink?"

They looked at him quickly, distrustfully. He laughed and said, "Now wait a minute. I'm a Yankee. On your side, remember?"

One said, "Ah, guess we could have another beer."

Burgess brought the steins, frowning, not knowing what to make of this, but he was determined to stay out of it. Heinz looked at the men more carefully and recognized two as having been in Dane's patrol at Slade's place.

"You made good time back," he said.

"De cap'n he don' like to fool around," one said.

"I didn't see your sergeant," Heinz said. "He on some other duty?"

The three policemen glanced at each other, then one said, "Oh, he go ovah de hill, boss. Skip out, dat's what he do."

"Now that's sure odd," Heinz said pleasantly. "You'd' think a fellow after working so hard for those stripes would think a little more of them. Well, I suppose his bad luck's your good. One of you's liable to be promoted."

"Ah guess we jus' wait and see."

He was the talkative one, and Heinz turned all his attention to him. "What's your name?"

"Alexander."

"Well, with a name like that, a man could go places." He pointed to the beer. "Want those glasses topped?"

They shook their heads, then Alexander said, "The cap'n, he don' trust you."

"Sometimes I don't trust the captain," Heinz said gently. "But that don't mean we can't get along, does it? I mean, one good thing deserves another, doesn't it? I buy you some beer and you tell me who shot the sergeant, Slade or the boy?"

They weren't ready for the question and his answer was in their faces, in their eyes when they quickly looked at each other, and in their hands that reached for their holstered pistols.

Heinz jumped back, scooped up the Henry repeater and fanned the hammer, firing the cartridge he kept in the chamber. Alexander clapped both hands to his breast, staggered and fell and Heinz worked the lever, rolling off two more shots in rapid succession.

One of the policemen managed to get off a

shot, but he was late with it and the bullet punked into the sawdust on the floor. In a matter of seconds it was over and Burgess ran around the bar, holding his unfired shotgun.

He grabbed Heinz by the arm, rushed him into the back room and pushed him up through a hidden ceiling door that led into an attic. Then Burgess rushed out to the back entrance, smashed the door open with a lunge of his shoulder, and fired both barrels of his shotgun into the air.

By the time he got back to the bar, Dane was hurrying in, a handful of police with him. He looked at the dead men, then took the shotgun away from Burgess and said, "You're under arrest."

"I didn't do it," Burgess said. "They're pistol shot. Besides, I couldn't shoot three men with two barrels."

This calmed Dane and he examined the shotgun. "I heard this go off."

"Sure you did," Burgess said. "I took some shots at the bugger that did this."

"How did it happen?" Dane demanded.

"Well, I was down below the edge of the bar when the argument started. It flared quick, then I heard these shots—BANGBANGBANG! And another shot—I guess one of your boys got off one. When I looked up, this jasper was boltin' for the back of my place. Went right through my back door. That's the kind of a hurry he was in. So I grabbed up my shotgun and took out after him."

"I suppose you missed him?"

"I guess I did," Burgess said, shamefaced. "Sorry, captain. It just happened so damned fast though."

Dane made a motion with his hand. "Get these men out of here before the curious show up." He took Burgess by the arm and led him out of the way and the dead men were carried out. "Now I want you to think very carefully," Dane said, "and describe exactly the man who killed my men."

"Yes, sir," Burgess said, wrinkling his face. "Well, he was kind of short. Almost runty. And he had a broad face. Mexican blood I figured right off. Never seen him before though."

"How was he dressed?"

"Oh, hat, coat, pants, boo—"

"You idiot, I can guess that!" Dane snapped. "What kind of hat?"

"Kind of Mexican type. Big in the brim and tall in the crown."

"And the coat?"

"Kind of fur, like an old buffalo coat that had been cut off."

"You're no help at all," Dane said. "How did this man get to town?"

"I don't know, captain. Like I said, I didn't see him—"

"Yes, yes," Dane said impatiently. He went to the front door and opened it and looked out. "Who belongs to that horse tied there?"

Burgess swallowed hard. "Don't know."

Dane examined it and came back in. "No brand. Some range animal fresh broken to saddle." He looked around the room. "Not much to go on, but I'll hang somebody for it. What was the argument about?"

Burgess shook his head. "I really can't say. There wasn't much talk between parties, you might say. The policemen were talkin' among themselves, speculatin' on whether a white man hates 'em because they're dark or because they're police. The next thing I knew the shootin' started, BANGBANGBA—"

"You've gone through that, you fool," Dane said. "You close this place until further notice."

"You mean, I'm out of business?"

"Exactly," Dane said and stalked out.

Burgess locked the doors and blew out the lights and went in back, then tapped on the ceiling with a broom handle. Heinz came down and Burgess said, "Now what happened?"

"They were part of the bunch that murdered Fred Slade and his family."

Burgess swore. "Fred used to come in here now and then. Murdered, huh?"

"Yes, and you've got to get me a horse so I can ride to the post," Heinz said. "The colonel's got to know about this."

"About you shootin' those three?" Burgess shook his head. "Heinz, you've got to figure out some other way. Dane means to hang someone

110

and he don't need much of an excuse to pick on you."

"Can you get me out of town?"

"That I can do," Burgess said.

11

The murder of Fred Slade's family was news and it spread fast, passed from one rider to another until everyone knew that the police had done it, and that three of them had paid for it, and maybe the sergeant too, and men who moved around the prairie constantly kept looking for a grave, or listening to rumor of a wounded man hiding out.

Colonel Shannon came to the Pritchard place and was taken to the drawing room and word was sent out to Carl Heinz, who was away from the ranch at the time. He arrived after the evening meal and found Shannon in a foul frame of mind.

"I'm going to ask you one question, Heinz, and I want an honest answer," Shannon said, as soon as Heinz closed the study door. "All I've heard is accusations against the police. Who killed those three policemen in Burgess' place?"

Heinz glanced at General Nathan Pritchard, then said, "I did."

"Oh, come on—" He stopped and looked carefully at Heinz. "Carl, this is impossible. My God, man, you're a civilized—I mean, you wouldn't take the law in your own hands."

"Why shouldn't I, colonel? What other law is there?"

Shannon puffed his cheeks. "With this admission I could arrest you and try you and have you hung."

"I didn't hear any admission," General Pritchard said gently.

Shannon glanced at him, then nodded. "I see how it is."

"No, I'm afraid you don't," Pritchard said. "But I'll tell you, suh, exactly how it is. The police are as bad as any outlaws that ever plagued Texas. I do not speak in generalities, because I've heard that in some districts they are doing a good job and not harassing the people. I'm speaking of here, suh, right under your nose, and under your command."

"That's unfair, general!"

"Unfair, suh? Hell, man, you put it mildly. I can offer no reason why Slade's family was killed. Had he alone been shot I would have suspected that he'd flung an insult at one of those men, but there was no reason for the woman and boy to die. Unless it served some purpose of Dane's."

"What reason could Dane have?" Shannon asked. "General, the man's name is getting pretty black."

"Black hardly describes it," Pritchard said. He

glanced at Carl Heinz. "The two of us have discussed this, colonel. We'd like to offer our opinion."

"I'll listen to it," Shannon said. "Beyond that—"

"Of course, of course," Pritchard said, waving his hand. "We know that Caleb Early is kin to Dane. You know it too, or you've heard it said. Early is here to buy cattle, to make a lot of money, but he's run into stubborn Texas pride. Many of us, general, would starve, yes, let our families starve before we'd take money from someone we hated. Dane and Early know that and I think that they did something about it." He leaned forward in his chair and looked intently at Shannon. "They killed the Slade family in cold blood so that others will think about it when Early comes around with his cattle offer, and the next time, it'll be at his price."

Shannon's face mirrored his shock. "General, that's a terrible accusation. And completely unfounded."

"We don't think so," Heinz said frankly. "We know that Dane and some of his policemen did the killing at the Slade place. If we ever find that sergeant—"

"He's going to be found," Pritchard said. "This is our country and we know every rabbit warren where a man could hide." He looked at Shannon. "General, let's talk facts. If you had to gather your command tomorrow and march against us

Texans, what chance do you think you'd have of licking us?"

Shannon chewed on his lip and said, "Frankly, general, not too good."

"You have a token army, suh," Pritchard pointed out. "Occupation of enemy territory is done really with the consent of the enemy; you would have to outnumber us by a goodly amount otherwise. I'm going to be honest with you, suh. We're tired of Dane and his police. Not tired of law and order, but tired of abuse, incompetence, and his brand of justice. We no longer care to bow to his law, suh."

"General, I can't see that you have any choice," Shannon said.

"We have an alternative," Pritchard said, "and we're prepared to take it. We can fight. Is that what you want, colonel? A war? By God, we can give you a bloody one and win it in the end." He counted the points he wanted to make on the tips of his fingers. "One: The law that even Dane must bow to, and you, suh, is a United States Marshal. We want one here."

"It would take months to get one here," Shannon said.

"Not if you had a man here that could be sworn in by proxy," Pritchard said. "Two: We want a review of the laws enacted since the war, and a voice in their revision."

"General, I couldn't justify that to my superiors."

"Three: If we don't get these reasonable demands,

114

suh, you can gird your loins for battle because we're serving notice on Dane and every man in his command. I can allow you ten days, no longer."

Shannon rubbed a hand across his face. "Suppose I said I'd do these things. Who's going to be the marshal and enforce these laws?"

"Carl Heinz," Pritchard said. "Pick me a better man, suh."

Shannon thought about it, then shook his head. "I guess I couldn't. General, how about a little give in the deal. If I can secure an appointment for Carl, would you consent if he acted as your spokesman in any lawmaking sessions that might be necessary?"

"We have complete faith in him," Pritchard said.

Shannon sat down and put a match to a cigar. "General, you understand what you're doing? You're rushing things, trying to get out from under a legal governorship."

"I am trying, suh, to get some protection, some justice for my people," Pritchard said flatly. "Colonel, your troops are in no way effective. Instead of watching us, they ought to be watching the police."

"If it wasn't Dane, who would you complain about?" Shannon asked, then waved his hand, not really wanting an answer. He looked at Carl Heinz. "You killed three policemen. Tell me what difference there is between you and the outlaw, Hardin?"

"I did it because there was no other way to touch them," Heinz said. "Colonel, would it have done any good to come to you with the truth? Would you have acted?" He shook his head. "You don't give justice to these people. It's as much your fault as anyone's. Give a man a reasonable recourse of law and he won't take matters to himself. I don't praise Hardin, but I don't blame him. He has no other way to fight. Yes, he's wrong and he'll hang someday, not because he killed a couple of policemen, but because he couldn't stop killing once he started."

Shannon thought about this. "You may be right, Carl. I don't say that I did what was good for Texas, but what was good for me, what my superiors would approve of. There are powerful men in Washington who want to punish the south. You want self administration. They don't want that. And they'll have their say."

"Money talks," Pritchard said. "Texas money will change their minds." He took a final drag on his cigar and snuffed it out. "I've received word that a man in north Texas is planning a cattle drive in the spring. Others will follow, colonel. Those Yankee politicians can only see prairie now, but once the cattle move north they'll see money here and their attitude will change. When can I expect word on the establishment of some reasonable law around here?"

"You mean, when can you have some law of your own."

"Put it any way you want," Pritchard said. "Carl's a just man. You trust him, and so do we."

"I believe I can meet your demand in ten days," Shannon said, then stopped talking and turned his head because there was a commotion in the yard. Someone fired a weapon several times and Pritchard vaulted out of his chair and went to the door leading to the porch.

"What the devil's going—" He stopped yelling and stared at the two bearded men flinging off by the hitching post. "Nix! Owen!"

They came to the porch, laughing; Nix had one arm in a sling and his clothes were ripped and he hadn't had a bath for a month. Owen Pritchard carried saddlebags and he tossed them to his father, who caught and staggered under the weight.

"You just count them Yankee dollars," Owen said, and they went into the house.

Both men stood in the study and looked at the ceiling while the general poured the drinks. Nix said, "That's the first roof I've seen in forty days." He took the whiskey and downed it, then blew out his breath. "The rest of the men ain't more'n four days behind us."

"What's the matter with your arm?" the general asked.

"Got it bullet broke," Nix said. He flopped into a chair and stretched his legs. His boots were split at the seams and his chaps were ruined; about these men there was nothing that had not been brutally used. They were thinned, tougher, and immensely pleased with themselves. "In all, we lost close to a hundred and fifty head in stampedes, rivers, and to Indian trouble." He looked at Carl Heinz. "The railroad was there, just like you said, and three buyers. They met us four days out and I closed the deal for thirty-one dollars a head."

Owen reached out and punched the saddlebags with his fist. "Me and the Leslie boys went on into town ahead of the herd, Pa." He shook his head. "You talk about Texas bein' wild. Every card sharp had his deck ready to take the boys' wages. But they didn't get as much as they figured because I'd only paid them one month's pay. There was a little trouble over that. Guns came into play and before it was over, Nix got hit in the arm." He reached inside his shirt and brought out a soiled notebook. "The accounts have been kept, Pa, and they'll come here to be paid."

"We lost six men," Nix said. "Countin' the ones that got shot. I guess we can pay the full amount to their families, including the bonus."

"Certainly," the general said. "It's too bad we couldn't have thought of that contingency before you left. It would have saved argument and lives."

Nix turned his head and looked at Colonel Shannon. "Saw some army there, colonel. What for I wouldn't know. The Yankee bandits jumped us ten miles south of town, meanin' to relieve us of all that cash, of course. They got more of a fight than they figured on. Couldn't say how many got hurt, but by the time the army arrived, we were headin' south." He took one of his father's cigars and lit it. "We ran into the other outfit about fifteen days out and warned them to be on the lookout for the border jumpers. Them Yankees figure they've got a good thing, lettin' us drive the cattle, then they'll steal 'em close to Abilene."

"I have to send a dispatch rider north anyway," Shannon said. "I'll make a formal request to the commanding officer to use his troops if necessary to stop this activity."

Owen Pritchard laughed. "Colonel, you're wastin' your time. Those toughs are runnin' the army ragged. They're organized and next year it'll be worse. A man will not only have to drive a herd a thousand miles but fight a war when he gets there in order to reach the market." He looked at his father. "Where are the girls?"

"They took the buggy in town," the general said. "Why don't you boys clean up and try a bed for a change. I'll get the word around that the men are coming back. We'll have a blowout this week end."

Both men had another glass of whiskey, then left the study and the general lit a fresh cigar. "If the others are as ragged as they are—" He glanced at Heinz and laughed. "We'll have to better equip the next outfit."

"Yes, we can afford it," Heinz said. "General, may I offer some advice? By tomorrow morning, Captain Dane's going to know this money is here. Place a strong guard around it."

Shannon sputtered with sudden anger. "Really, Carl, that remark was unfounded and completely uncalled for!"

"That may be your opinion, sir, but I wouldn't trust Dane out of my sight."

Pritchard said, "I'll take your advice, Carl. Sorry, colonel, but I share his opinion. Dane has killed. He'll rob too."

"The whole idea offends me," Shannon said. "Damn it, sir, we pick our officers more carefully than—"

"He's no officer and never will be," Heinz said. "Can't you admit your contempt for the man?"

"Not while he wears a uniform," Shannon said.

"That can change," Heinz said and went to his room. He changed into his riding clothes, took his rifle and a belt of ammunition and went to the barn and saddled a horse. He told one of the hands where he was going and rode north, following the trail in the snow the Pritchard boys had left.

He camped the night in a rocky draw and enjoyed a lonely fire, and in the morning he was riding again. Before noon he saw the men riding toward him and he fired his rifle twice, then galloped over to them.

The Leslie boys recognized him and hauled him off the horse and wrestled him in the snow and finally he pinned Ed face down and made him give up.

Heinz had never seen so ragged a group of men, but if it ever came to picking men, he would gladly have singled out each one. Ed Leslie pounded him on the back and waved his Henry repeater.

"You should have seen them border bandits when they ran into these repeaters. We gave 'em a volley and they charged us, thinkin' they'd catch us reloadin'. Man, we cut 'em down like brush."

"Don't you men ever shave?" Heinz asked, looking them over.

One grinned. "Mister, we ain't seen a razor since Abilene. And when the wind's right, you can tell we ain't seen a bath either."

They had questions to ask him, about their families, and he tried to answer them all. Every man was jumping to get home and the smell of home was in the air, a yearning in their eyes and the impatient way they sat their saddles. Behind them were the dangers and the trouble and Heinz supposed if they had to turn around and go back now not one would do it.

But in the spring they'd feel differently.

They'd go again in the spring.

12

Winter was a succession of brief snows, and thaws, and a lot of wind; it was a time of the year that men waited out for the real work always began in the spring. General Pritchard's celebration of the completed trail drive was a magnet that drew people for miles around, and on Carl Heinz' advice, Pritchard invited Captain Dane and his officers and Caleb Early; Heinz operated on the theory that it was always best to have the enemy where he could be observed.

Most of the officers from the post came to Pritchard's place, and with proper urging, Colonel Shannon announced that he was granting an appointment to the post of United States Marshal; Carl Heinz was sworn in and badged and the air was punctured with gunshots and rebel yells. The Texans liked it, but Captain Dane didn't.

He and his cousin left early.

At the first opportunity, Heinz and Shannon went into the house and enjoyed a cigar in the general's study.

"I'll have to draw on your general fund, colonel," Heinz said. "I want to build an office and jail in town."

"What's wrong with the post stockade?"

"Nothing, and I'll probably transfer prisoners

there," Heinz said. "But it's too far away for ready access." He smiled. "I'll also need your signature on a voucher authorizing the salaries for two deputies."

Shannon frowned. "Let's not be a peasant drunk with power."

"I think you're glad to do it," Heinz said. "What's a hundred and sixty a month in salaries and say five hundred dollars for building costs if it gets the job done?" He took his cigar from his mouth and pointed with it. "You're too smart a man to hamstring me. If I do the job, you'll get the credit for it. Perhaps some eastern post or staff in Washington. We'll both get what we want."

"Just what do we want, Carl?" He looked sharply at Heinz. "Something noble?"

"No, I don't think so," Heinz said. "You don't like this command; no one would. I didn't like it either. But I like Texas. I think it's a place of opportunity and you won't have to tear it apart to make a go of it either. Quite the contrary. I think a man will make the most of it by building. I like a dollars and cents profit as well as the next man, but I'm not after a quick dollar. To insure my good fortune, I have to insure the good fortune of Texas. Follow me?"

"All the way," Shannon said. He fell silent for a moment. "I'll call a meeting at the post in the middle of next week. Dane will be there. He won't like any of this."

123

"We don't need the police," Heinz said. "Reactivate the Texas Rangers in this section if you want a law enforcement body. But get rid of those Negro police."

"How can I justify that to my superiors, Carl?" Shannon asked. "This plan was drawn up in Wash—"

"I know, and maybe it would have been better if they'd come here for a look around first," Heinz said. "Did we fight a war for the privilege of grinding a heel in someone's face?" He shook his head. "As I see it, the flaw is that Negro police can't do the job in Texas, or anywhere else in the south right now. They've been put into an impossible position. Someone, somewhere has to admit the error and do something about it. Colonel, you govern a lot of square miles of Texas. You're the supreme authority. I'm appealing to that authority to give me six months to establish just law and order. If I succeed, I want Dane and his command to be the hell and gone clear of Texas."

"That leaves me with the job of justifying that to my superiors," Shannon said.

"I think you can do that," Heinz said.

Shannon smiled. "You credit me with persuasive powers I may not possess." He reached out and slapped Heinz on the knee. "I think you could have been a general if you'd stayed with it."

"There are all kinds of generals, sir," Heinz said. He did not go outside with Shannon, but went into the great living room looking for Nan. He found her by one of the windows, looking out; she turned her head when he closed the door and he went over to her and kissed her.

"I don't see enough of you," she said and touched the badge pinned to his vest. "I think now I may see even less." She looked at the people in the yard. "You did this, Carl."

"No, they did it. Next year they'll drive north, your father and many others. In the spring you'll see new faces in Texas because the farmers will start coming in, and the land speculators and the grabbers. They always wait for someone to show them the way." He went to the sideboard and poured two glasses of wine and brought one to her, then stood by the window and looked out. "There's more here than cattle, Nan. We've got to open up the country before it busts its britches. People are on the move everywhere. That means stage lines and freight lines and new towns and new business. A man doesn't sit back and let it happen. He goes out and makes it happen."

"Is that what you're going to do?" she asked.

"Yes, if my luck holds out." He bent and touched his glass to hers and they drank to that.

As soon as his office was built, Carl Heinz hired two deputy marshals: Ed and Joe Leslie, who helped supervise the construction of the jail, and since the government was paying for it, Heinz had a stout building erected. He put everything on a vacant lot at the end of the street where no one could miss it. Come into town one way and you saw it ahead of you. Come in the other and you had to pass it. The jail was stone, two stories, with the offices and housekeeping rooms to one side. Twice Colonel Shannon came to watch the progress of construction.

Caleb Early also paid attention, but quietly, from his hotel room overlooking the street, and when Paul Dane came to town they sat there and looked at the building.

"I've made up my mind," Dane said. "I'm getting out of it. Shannon has reduced my effectiveness by appointing Heinz marshal. I haven't any more authority."

"I want you to stick with it," Early said. "There's too much invested to let it go. The boys up north are all set to hit the herds as they come through, and—"

"And they got the hell kicked out of them," Dane said fretfully. "Cal, somehow this isn't coming off like we planned."

"Give it time to shake down," Early said. "The boys are like soldiers; they need time to season up. Come spring they'll be better organized. That fellow Goodnight who's going to drive will run into some hot company." He reached out and tapped Dane on the arm. "And it's about time we started making some offers. I don't want anyone to forget what happened to the Slades."

126

"That was a dirty mess," Dane said. "I didn't like any of it." He glanced at Early. "I've had to be damned careful since then. When the sergeant got killed, my men didn't like it; he was a favorite. And then those three got plugged in Burgess' place. I don't think I could do a thing like that again. They wouldn't follow me."

"They may not have to," Early said. "The threat alone can do it." He put a match to his cigar. "Maybe you ought to get out at that, Paul. Why don't you go on north and handle it from that end for awhile?"

"You want to get rid of me?"

Early thought about this, then said, "If you don't back up, I may not have any choice. It's no good for a man to come apart, Paul."

"Hell, I'm all right," Dane snapped. "If you want to get rid of someone, get rid of Heinz."

"I'm working on that," Early said. "He's not bullet proof, you know."

"Make sure I'm not mixed up in it," Dane said. "I don't know what's got into Colonel Shannon, but he sure as hell doesn't trust me. He's all but gelded my police force. Do you know that I can't even make an arrest without turning the prisoner over to the marshal? I even have to clear my warrants through his office." He blew through his nose. "Someday I'll have my chance with Heinz, alone."

"Well, Texas is going back to the Texans," Caleb Early said. "Of course, we both knew it was bound to happen. All we have to do is to see that some of it goes to us." He stopped talking as a buggy came into town, then he smiled as Nan Pritchard got down. She said something to her sister, then the driver turned, cut across the street and parked in front of the hotel while Nan went into the store. Early got up and said, "You use the back way. I'll go see if I can't strike up a conversation with Miss Pritchard."

"You ought to leave her alone," Dane said. "She's a Pritchard and—"

"And that makes her all the more attractive to me," Early said, smiling. "The Pritchards have money now." He stepped out, adjusted his tie, then went down the stairs.

She was at the desk, talking to the clerk, and he came up, smiling, hat in hand. He was sure she wouldn't recall his brief visit to the ranch when the general celebrated the safe delivery of the first herd. "Miss Pritchard, I regret that until this moment I haven't had the pleasure of meeting you. I'm Caleb Early." He offered his hand and she took it hesitatingly. "Unfortunately business commitments have prevented me from calling at your home to pay my respects."

"Why would you want to do that?" Cecilia Pritchard asked, her manner frank, but reserved.

"Because I intend to make my home in Texas," Early said. "Is there any reason why we couldn't be friends?"

"No," she said. "And of course there's no reason why we should."

"Except that you're a very attractive woman." he said. "Are you staying in town overnight?"

"Yes."

"Then perhaps you'll have dinner with me? At eight?"

"I'm having dinner in my room," she said.

"Well, I suppose it was too much to expect," Early said.

Cecilia smiled. "Really, Mr. Early, you've dined alone before."

He laughed softly. "That wasn't what I meant. I was thinking that it was too much to expect the Pritchard nerve to be also present in the female line of the family."

"So you're challenging me," Cecilia said.

He nodded. "I hope, when you know me better, you'll forgive me for it."

"Just so that we understand each other," she said, "you've used a man's trick on me. I feel free to use a woman's."

"Acceptable terms," Early said. "At eight?"

"Exactly at eight," she said. "Now if you'll excuse me?" She brushed past him and went on up the stairs and before he went out he winked at the clerk.

Nan Pritchard left the store and walked to the end of the street to the marshal's office and found Ed Leslie mopping the floor. He stepped into a short hall and whistled and a moment later Carl

Heinz came down the stairs from the upper cell block.

"Let's have some coffee, Ed," he said, then scooted a chair around so that she could sit down. "How do you like my bastion of law and order? It's a bit empty at the moment, but I expect to have boarders in it soon."

"It would take a cannon to knock it down," she said. "Cecilia and I are going to stay overnight. If the mountains won't come to—"

"I know," he said. "Being busy sounds like a bad excuse. Has anyone found a trace of Dane's sergeant?"

She shook her head. "Nix was talking about it. He says he doesn't think the man is dead. Either that, or he wasn't buried on the prairie."

"He's dead," Heinz said. "Dane made a mistake, an oversight. The word's around that the sergeant went over the hill, deserted. If that's so, why didn't Dane put out a wanted notice on him?" He shook his head. "The sergeant may not be on the prairie. He may be somewhere in Marfa, right on the police post."

"Carl, why is the sergeant so important? If he's dead he can't testify."

"No, but I can bring Dane in and sweat the truth out of him. That would make two lies I'd have caught him in. One, that the sergeant deserted, and two, how a man could be buried under his nose and he not know it."

"Getting Dane is an obsession, isn't it?"

He shrugged. "I'd rather not think it was. Maybe it is. It wouldn't make any difference anyway. Nan, the colonel thinks I'm an idealist. Honestly, I think he's wrong. A man's motives can sound idealistic, and actually be very practical. I want to make something of my life, and financial success is a part of it. But I want it to be good, good for me and for everyone. There is enough Yankee in me to see the justice of making a profit as long as others aren't cut out of it. I know Dane. He's the kind who once bought an acre of land from the Indian for a plug of tobacco, then shot him because he walked across it. In another time and place, other men would decide the merits of men like Dane and Early. But now I have to take the responsibility onto myself. Only I'll surrender it when the time comes. Your father's like that. He owns a big part of Texas, Nan, and he has a big say in how things will go."

"There's something I've been thinking about," Nan said. "Captain Dane isn't very brave. He'd shoot a man in the back."

"He's already figured out a way to get the job done for him," Heinz said. He reached into his desk drawer and pulled out a stack of warrants. "Dane turned these over to me to be served. You'll notice that he's put Wesley Hardin's right on top."

"Hardin will never surrender without a fight!"

131

"And I can't begin to match Hardin with a pistol," Heinz said. "But that's a murder warrant, for the killing of that Negro policeman. If I don't serve it, what good is this badge?"

"Dane wants Hardin to kill you."

Heinz nodded. "Well, I'm going to give him a chance. For a week now I've spread the word, hoping it'll reach Hardin, offering to meet him any place he chooses." He tapped the stack of warrants. "Of all the men wanted here, Hardin is the most important. He's got to be brought in."

13

Carl Heinz didn't time it that way, but it was the way things worked out; the general's second trail herd got through and the men came back and the celebration was planned and Heinz got word that Wesley Hardin would be there.

This was no implied challenge and everyone knew it; Hardin was posting his notice that he intended to do what he pleased, when he pleased and they watched Heinz to see what he was going to do about it. Or perhaps those who knew him well understood what he was going to do and only waited to see it.

The general hosted the affair; his home was the focal point for miles around and the day the beef went into the pits, people began to gather, in wagons and buggies and on horseback and many afoot. The winter's cold was broken and some snow remained in patches, but the days were turning sunny and the weather was mild and here and there brave patches of grass began to show signs of growth.

The Leslie boys went out to the Pritchard place with orders to keep out of trouble and they knew what Heinz meant, but late in the evening Joe Leslie came back to town and found Heinz asleep on the cot.

He shook him awake and said, "Hardin showed up."

"Time to go then," Heinz said and pulled on his boots.

"He ain't the same man at all," Leslie said. "A real hard one."

"Didn't you expect that?" Heinz put on his coat and picked up his Henry repeater, dropping a handful of cartridges in his pocket. "I don't expect any favors, Joe. Hardin figures he owes no one anything." He looked at Leslie. "Fetch my horse, will you?"

"This could wait until morning," Leslie said.

Heinz smiled. "I want to be there in the morning."

He locked the office and waited on the board-walk while Leslie went to the stable, then when the man came back, Heinz stepped into the saddle and they rode out of town together.

By his calculations, Heinz figured to arrive at the Pritchard place a little before midnight, and normally most everyone would have been bedded down for the night, but he found the fires bright and people up and about.

Joe Leslie said, "They knew you were coming."

"We don't want to disappoint anybody," Heinz said and dismounted in the center of the camp. He did this to give people a chance to see him riding in, and to give Hardin a chance. There was no other way to take the man except in front of these people because Hardin needed witnesses when he defied the law, and Heinz needed them when he enforced it.

He handed the reins to Joe and said, "Find Ed and get out of sight. You two stay out of it, do you hear?"

"You're a fool," Joe Leslie said. "Hardin's a crack shot and he can get his pistol in a hurry."

"You do what I tell you or you go back to riding for somebody," Heinz said. He walked over to a big fire and took off his gloves and warmed his hands. He put the gloves in a side pocket and stood with the Henry cradled in his arm. There were a half a hundred people around this fire and more gathered, as though it spread some unusual warmth. Heinz waited, looking round, but saying nothing. He kept his heavy buffalo coat buttoned to the neck and turned down an offer of coffee.

Then he saw some men in the back stir and it

was like a sea of grass disturbed by some small animal; their heads and shoulders moving as Wesley Hardin passed through.

When he reached the inner row he stopped and stood there, hands relaxed at his sides. He wore no coat, just a vest over his light shirt. Around his waist were two crossed leather belts with holstered pistols, their butts forward; he did not touch them but his hands were not far from them. The people behind Heinz remained rooted while those behind Hardin moved away and Heinz was not encouraged by the implication that Hardin wouldn't miss while his bullet went wild.

"You're looking for me?" Hardin said, making it only a half question.

"You know I have a warrant," Heinz said.

For a moment Hardin stared, then he said, "You must be a fool to think you can serve it."

"I have to serve it," Heinz said calmly. "If anyone's a fool, it's you. Why don't you submit to arrest and stand trial? Do you think there's a jury in Texas who'd convict you for killing that policeman? Why don't you use your head and clean the slate instead of making a braggart's fight of it?"

"You're scared," Hardin said. "Tryin' to talk your way out of it?"

"I'm trying to talk you out of dangling at the end of a rope," Heinz said. "Hardin, how many chances do you think a man has?"

"You've used up yours," Hardin said. "I've paid you back for the favor you did me by not killing that police captain. Now you either crawl out of here or start shooting."

"You know what I have to do," Heinz said and swung up the rifle.

Hardin drew his portside pistol and fired twice before Heinz could bring the Henry level and both bullets struck Heinz high in the chest, spinning him, knocking him down, and he hit and rolled and worked the lever of the Henry, firing once, the bullet breaking Hardin's shoulder.

The young gunman staggered, clapped a hand to his bleeding wound, and stared at the man who should have been dead; Heinz was slowly, painfully getting to his feet. Then Hardin swore and reached for his other gun, but stopped when Heinz said, "I'll break your other shoulder!"

The gunman stopped with his fingers curled around the butt, then he hooked it out of the holster by the trigger guard and tossed it on the ground. Heinz staggered a little when he walked over and kicked both weapons away, and the people stared at him because he couldn't be doing this; no man could take two slugs in the chest and walk around as though nothing had happened.

From his pocket, Heinz produced a pair of handcuffs and snapped them on Hardin's wrist, then he looked around for the Leslie boys and found them standing nearby. "Take him in the house and see if anyone can get that bullet out of his shoulder," Heinz said.

They came forward and Hardin said, "Wait! Mister, I hit you twice."

"Yes you did," Heinz said. "But I never knew a .36 Colt that would shoot through a good buffalo coat, a suit coat, and a vest." He nodded to Joe and Ed Leslie. "Take him inside."

Heinz should have done this himself, but this was showmanship, a part of the job, and he turned to the fire. "I'll take that coffee now."

A dozen men moved to the pot and he took a cup and gingerly sipped it. Jess Windridge said, "Marshal, you'd have been out of luck if he'd been packing .44s."

"Hardin likes the .36 Colt," Heinz said. "I counted on that."

One man laughed. "After tonight he won't like 'em."

They all thought this was funny, but Windridge was serious. "It's like I was sayin' all along: you get one good man on the job and you can get rid of them police."

Heinz drank some more of his coffee, then put the cup down. "Have a good time," he said and pushed his way through and walked toward the house. He didn't feel that he was out of sight until he reached the dark part of the porch, and there he stopped and leaned against the post and unbuttoned his coat and vest and put his hand inside where his shirt was sticky with blood. There was a solid, aching pain in his chest and he had trouble breathing freely, but with some effort he straightened and went on in, using the side door that went through the library. He found a servant and motioned for him to come over.

"Ask Miss Nan to come in here, please." Then he closed the door and slumped in the general's leather chair. A few minutes later Nan hurried in. "Lock the door," Heinz said.

"Joe told me—"

"Never mind what Joe told you," Heinz said. "Can you draw those curtains and lock the outside door?" She nodded and did this, then he turned up the lamp. He could see her face clearly, the concern there, and he took her hand. "Nan, listen to me. I didn't get off as lucky as most think. Both Hardin's bullets went through the coat. I can feel them lodged right under the skin." She gasped and he quieted her by shaking his head. "Get some whiskey and a sharp knife and clean cloth and take care of this for me. And no servants. No one's to know." He smiled. "It's part of the legend of invincibility we have to have in this job." He tightened his grip on her hand. "Now you're not going to cry or anything like that, are you?"

She took a deep breath. "No, I'll be all right."

After she went out, Heinz poured a stiff one from the general's private bottle and downed it.

Then she came back and locked the door and helped him off with his coat. She had one of her brother's shirts and laid this aside.

The bullets were not two inches apart, lodged in the left pectoral muscle and had it been summer time, he'd be stone dead. "That guy can shoot," Heinz said as she cleaned the wound with whiskey. He breathed heavily and was glad when she picked up the knife. The wounds were shallow and not at all serious and they were numb; she got both bullets out, made a final cleaning, then bandaged him well.

He had another whiskey, then put on the shirt and finished dressing while she burned his soiled shirt and clothes in the fireplace. Heinz walked around and found the pain bearable. He said, "This has been a good night, Nan."

"Good? You almost got yourself killed, that's how good it was." She wanted to be a woman, to cry a little, and to fuss and ask him to give it all up, but she held it back. "I didn't know you were here until I heard the shots. Then the Leslie boys brought Hardin into the house."

"Where is he?"

"In the servants' quarters off the kitchen," she said.

"I think I'll go talk to my prisoner," Heinz said and kissed her. Instead of letting her go, he held her, and said, "You're a real woman, Nan. All a man could want."

"If you're not careful, I may be a widow before I'm married," she said.

He walked to the rear of the house and saw the Leslies standing by a closed door. "It's a storeroom," Ed said. "He can't get out."

"Did you get the bullet out of him?"

"Yep," Joe said. "He's a little groggy from the whiskey."

"Unlock the door," Heinz said and stepped inside. Hardin was stretched out on a cot and a lamp was on a nearby table; he turned his head and looked steadily at Heinz.

"You're the first man that ever put a bullet in me," he said.

Heinz toed a chair around and sat down. "There'll be others. You can't keep a pistol in the holster."

Hardin laughed. "Not if they hang me."

"They won't hang you," Heinz said. "A little time in jail maybe, but not the rope. Things have changed."

"How much time in jail?"

Heinz shrugged. "That's up to Colonel Shannon. He'll be trying the case."

"I don't like jail," Hardin said.

"You'll like it better than the rope," Heinz told him. "Why don't you cut this out, Hardin? Settle down. Run cattle or chase women or something."

"I like my life."

"How many men have you killed?"

"Seven."

Heinz nodded. "Now this is an important question: How many of them were Texans like yourself?"

"Six," Hardin said. "What about it? They were all fair fights."

"What's fair against a man as good with a pistol as you?" Heinz asked. "Hardin, you'd better get this through your skull: You may think you're doing right. You're not. You're turning into a shooter and pretty soon these people are going to see the tarnish on you."

"Texans stick together."

"You're a damned fool if you believe that," Heinz said. "Hardin, in the beginning, that night I gave you my gun and my horse, you may have been a misguided young man fighting an injustice and people helped you because they felt that injustice too. But you can wear that out. You can lose sight of it until those same people will turn against you because they can't go on living with a dangerous man among them. Now you think about that."

"They were for me tonight," Hardin said. "There wasn't a man here who would have helped you."

"No, you're wrong. Joe and Ed Leslie would have shot you down like a mad dog if I hadn't ordered them to stand clear of it," Heinz said. "And those people who saw this business weren't for you. They were afraid to go against your gun, but they weren't for you. Hardin, you've come to a crossroad. Better take the right one or Texas won't want you. There's no place for you, if you go on this way."

"A man can make his place," Hardin said. "There's others like me."

"I know. I've got warrants and posters in my desk drawer. And one by one, we'll take you all in. Do you believe that?"

"No."

Heinz stood up. "Then look at yourself. The big pistol man, Wesley Hardin, laying on a cot with a broken shoulder. You thought you could win them all. No man can."

"You can't win 'em all either."

"I know. But when I try, I'm trying to do the right thing."

Heinz turned to the door and stepped out and Joe Leslie locked the door. "I want to leave first thing in the morning," Heinz said. "Ask the general if we can borrow a wagon." He stepped down the hall and the Leslies walked with him.

Ed said, "I could hear through the door, Carl. Maybe it would be best if Shannon hung him."

"He won't," Heinz said. "The military governor's attitude is changing. Hardin is a bowl of pap, so to speak. A year in jail is my guess."

"Then we do this all over again," Joe said. "Only next time he's going to be faster with his gun, and shoot straighter."

Heinz smiled thinly. "I guess I'll have to put in some practice, won't I?"

142

14

Ed Leslie arrested the Osmond brothers, three cattle thieves who had their headquarters forty miles south of Marfa, and Joe Leslie shot it out with Cal Singer and Morey Caslin in Alpine, Texas, two weeks later, killing one and badly wounding the other; the combination had a certain effect on some of the lawless elements and there was a noticeable surge of moving for less trouble-some climate.

Carl Heinz served nine warrants in twenty days and the top tier of cells in his jail were occupied and Colonel Shannon's calendar for trial dates was beginning to crowd up. Most of the offenses were minor; some of the charges were trumped up, Captain Dane's doing, and Heinz wanted them cleared or convicted, although he didn't think there was much chance of the latter.

Since his appointment as marshal, Paul Dane and his police had made no arrests, confining their activity to patrol duty, and this suited Heinz; he didn't want them to meddle for the bulk of his work as he saw it was clearing up the mess they'd made.

The success, if he was going to have any, would be measured not in the arrests he made, but in the attitude of the people toward him, and when they began to come to him with complaints and grievances to be settled, he knew that he had their trust, their confidence that he would dispense justice. Some things he settled according to his best judgment, and a few he turned over to Colonel Shannon.

Oliver Bassett, who ranched ten miles southeast of town, came in to Heinz's office late one evening and stood by the wall so he couldn't be seen from the street.

"I've been threatened," Bassett said. He was a short, whiskered man in rundown boots. Heinz had seen him before, when General Pritchard was trying to put together the second herd, but Bassett hadn't believed cattle could be driven so far and declined to go along with the drive.

"Sit down and tell me about it," Heinz said.

"I'll stand here. Don't want no one to see me," Bassett said. "Early's been to my place twice now. Wants to buy my cattle. I told him before I wouldn't sell. Going to join a trail herd in the spring. Now he wants to buy again, at half the price." He looked around. "Ain't nobody here but you and me, is there?"

"Prisoners upstairs," Heinz said. "Go on."

"The last time he made mention of what a terrible thing happened to the Slade family. Said it could happen again if a man wasn't careful. I got the idea right off. I either sell to him at his price or get burned out."

144

"How long did he give you to make up your mind?"

"Three days," Bassett said.

"Go on home to your family," Heinz said. "In a day or two we'll ride out and stay with you a spell. We'll be there sometime after dark. Keep this under your hat."

"Ain't about to say anything," Bassett said. "Was Early to find out I came here, I likely wouldn't get home."

"What kind of family do you have?"

"Wife, a daughter goin' on sixteen. Two boys a bit older."

Heinz nodded. "You pretty well armed?"

"Just what we managed to fetch home from the war," Bassett said.

"You go on home and don't worry about it. We'll be out there if trouble comes," Heinz said.

The man nodded and slipped out, and a moment later Carl Heinz followed him. He went to the saloon and found Ike Ball, who served as jailer, finishing his cold lunch and beer. Heinz gave him a ring of keys and said, "I'll be back tomorrow."

He got his horse from the stable, mounted and rode out of town, taking the post road. At a steady pace it was an all night ride, and with only a few rest stops he managed to raise the main gate by dawn. The sentry passed him through and he tied up in front of headquarters and stepped on the

145

porch as Colonel Shannon came from his quarters.

As Shannon came up he said, "I hope that orderly's made coffee," and went on inside, Heinz following him. The office stove threw out enough heat to push back the morning chill; a coffee pot steamed on the round top and Shannon poured two cups. "What jolly news have you brought me this time?"

"Remember the Slade family? There's going to be another."

Shannon looked up quickly. "The hell there is!"

"Dane and his men are going to hit the Bassett place in a few days. Early wants to buy Bassett's cattle, at his price. It makes sense now, why Slade was killed. Early is using that as an example of what can happen to a man and his family unless they do things his way. Dane will do the job. He and a squad of his police."

"Murder?"

Carl Heinz laughed. "Colonel, how many 'bullet' arrests have the police made in Texas? A hundred? Two hundred? A lot of Texans have died with police bullets in them. Those police troopers do what they're told. They're given a uniform and a badge and a gun and told to follow orders. I don't blame them. I blame Dane, and I'm going to get him this time."

"What do you want me to do?"

"First, I'll tell you what I'm going to do," Heinz said. "The Leslie boys and I will be in

146

Bassett's house, or around someplace. We'll do it quietly, when it's dark, and stay under cover. When Dane and his squad hits, we intend to give him more than he ever bargained for. Early gave Bassett three days. One's gone already. So it's day after tomorrow, probably in the evening just before sundown. You figure out the timing, sir, but have a full troop of cavalry moving in that area about that time. If Dane breaks away, I want someone who can give chase."

"I'll send Lieutenant Provine," Shannon said. "He's half Cherokee Indian and a better trail man I've never seen." He offered a cigar and lit one for himself. "Carl, I've received a few dispatches from governors in other sections of the country, and you're drawing a lot of attention to yourself and to me." He smiled. "Your appointment to marshal has been the first and they're watching to see how it works out. In fact, I'm expecting three commanders here for the hearings next month. They all seem dissatisfied with the police system and feel that it's unworkable and want to go back to something else, the Texas Rangers, or all US Marshals, or something other than what they have." He chuckled. "From the very first you've been against Paul Dane and his police. Frankly, I thought it was an unwarranted criticism. He did put down a lot of trouble, you know."

"He shot down a lot of men who were sore because they'd lost the war," Heinz said flatly.

Then he waved his hand. "What's the use to talk about it. I'll get Dane and once I have him cold no commander in Texas will be able to look at a police captain without suspicion. Colonel, I mean to break the back of that police force. Do you understand that? If I never do one more constructive thing I mean to rid Texas of this hideous miscarriage of political judgment."

Shannon went behind his desk and sat down. "I understand that you made a good little pot of money on the two cattle drives."

"I could have lost my shirt," Heinz said.

"Are you and the general still partners?"

"Yes, but I have no active part in the business. Nix and Owen have taken it over. We're committed to move fourteen thousand head north next year."

"One of these days," Shannon said, "when I'm retired at half pay, I'll stand on the sidewalk and watch you go by in your carriage. And if I pick up a rock and knock off your plug hat, you'll understand, won't you?" He sighed and puffed his cigar. "That's why I'm in the army, Carl; I have absolutely no business sense at all. An opportunity can step on my toes and I wouldn't recognize it." He leaned forward, elbows on the desk. "How do you do it, Carl? Tell the old man the secret."

"Well, I'm not sure I can," Heinz said. "You know how I used to ride in my spare time? Well, I'd see the country and look at the cattle and watch the people and it struck me that something had to move. The cattle had been breeding for four years and the range was getting choked. The market was north and the cattle were here and a lot of land lay between, but the laws of supply and demand have to be served. There was no other way but to drive to market. I'm sure they'd thought about it and worried about it, and all I did was push it into action. With or without me they'd have taken a herd north. It was bound to happen, only I wanted to be a part of it. That's opportunity."

"What else do you see?"

Heinz smiled. "Now I wouldn't want you resigning and beating me out of anything." He turned to the door. "Don't disappoint me day after tomorrow, colonel."

"I won't," Shannon said.

He rode back to Marfa, but made an overnight detour to Pritchard's place, had dinner with the general and his family, a cigar in the library afterward, and a few quiet hours with Nan. Heinz said nothing about the threat made against Bassett; the fewer who knew about it the better off they would be.

Before dawn he left and rode back to his office, arriving just before noon. Joe and Ed Leslie were in their bunks, sleeping off the rigors of a two day ride, and Heinz let them sleep. There was some mail on his desk and he went through that, and in the afternoon Captain Dane came in and sat down.

"I've been hoping you'd return in time," Dane said. "One of my patrols scouted a camp of outlaws about forty miles west of here the day before yesterday. In following your directive, no attempt was made to arrest them."

"How many in the party?"

"Three," Dane said. "My men recognized Ben Bickerstaff and the gunman they call Lee of Texas."

Carl Heinz whistled softly. "There's a pair for you. Thank you, captain. I appreciate your cooperation. Did your men observe the general direction these men were taking?"

"It seemed to be a permanent camp," Dane said. "My guess is that they're waiting to see how the Hardin affair comes out. He ran with them for awhile you know."

"That's likely the case," Heinz said. "All right, we'll take care of it."

Dane nodded and went out and Heinz got up and went to the window and watched him go down the street. Then he turned and found Ed Leslie standing in the doorway, batting his eyes to rid them of sleep.

"Does he have to talk so loud?"

"A common thing among small men," Heinz said. "Did you hear any of that?"

"Yeah," Ed Leslie said. "When do we leave?"

"We don't. There's no camp there."

Leslie frowned. "How's that?"

"Dane wants us on a goose chase," Heinz said,

150

and explained the threat made against Bassett. "In about an hour or so I want three horses saddled. Clean out the rifle rack and take along spare ammunition, and about three canteens of water. We'll mount up out front where Dane can see, and he'll be watching, then ride out as though we're going to raid that camp. After we clear town we'll make a big swing south and arrive at Bassett's place just after dark."

Ed Leslie smiled. "I'll wake Joe."

"Wait a minute. Go on down the street and bring Pete Burgess back here. I've got a job for him while we're gone."

Heinz sat at his desk and waited for Ed Leslie to come back, and a few minutes later Burgess opened the door and stepped inside. Ed came in and went into the other room and Burgess lowered his bulk into a chair.

"Pete, can you get together a gang of say fifteen men to do some digging and snooping for me?"

"Yeah. What's the job?"

"Dane and a squad of police will be leaving this evening and they'll be gone all night. Now we've never turned up that sergeant that was killed at Slade's place, and it's important that he be found. Personally, I think he's buried right here in town, somewhere around the police barracks or in the yard. I want him found even if you have to dig the whole place up."

Burgess nodded. "There'll be eight or ten

police still there. What do we do about those?"

"Can't you take care of them without shooting?"

Burgess smiled "Why, I guess we can, marshal. Consider it done."

Heinz pointed his finger. "I want that sergeant found, or what's left of him. Dane says he deserted. That's a lie. He was killed by one of the Slades and the body hidden. I've got to find him before I can call Dane a liar in court."

"If he's there, we'll find him," Burgess said. He stood up, then hesitated. "What's up anyway?"

"Maybe the end of the road," Heinz said. "Some luck has come our way. A man came to me and told me his troubles, Pete."

"Well I don't understand that."

"You will," Heinz said.

After Burgess went out, Heinz went into the living quarters and found the Leslie boys changing clothes. They were not the same men who had once stopped him on the street looking for trouble. Their hellishness was gone, replaced now with a seriousness that went with their responsibilities. Heinz knew that if he died tomorrow, either of them would make a better law officer than he had been.

Both of them had taken to wearing a pair of pistols and they kept them pushed to the front where they would be handy to get at. And Heinz, since his run in with Wes Hardin, had been wearing one just forward of his left hip; the

Leslie boys were coaching him in how to get it out of the holster without taking all afternoon, but with only slight success; Heinz liked the rifle, felt at home with it and was deadly with it.

Joe Leslie said, "I guess it's too much to expect that Caleb Early's goin' to be in on this."

"You can't have everything," Heinz said. "Once we get Dane in a cell upstairs, I've got a can of salt to put on Early's tail." He looked at each of them. "If you get a bead on Dane, just put him down. But I want him alive if it's possible."

"A man's hand can slip," Ed Leslie said.

"You're a deputy marshal," Heinz pointed out. "You enforce the law, not execute it."

"Like those three Negroes you shot in Burgess' place?"

Heinz let a bleakness come into his eyes. "I'll have that to live with and it's not good. I went off the handle, and no matter what the reasons I thought I had, I wish it hadn't happened. Don't make the same mistake." He reached out and slapped Ed on the shoulder. "Let's go."

15

There was no sign of life around Oliver Bassett's place when the three marshals arrived, but when they rode into the yard, Bassett thrust the muzzle of his rifle out a window and said,

"Stand fast or I'll blow you to kingdom come!"

"It's Heinz. Put up the gun and turn on those lamps."

One of Bassett's sons opened the door and Ed Leslie put up the horses while Carl Heinz and Joe Leslie went inside. "I didn't think it would be smart to show light," Bassett said.

"And tip Dane off that you were ready for him?" Heinz asked. "Turn the lamps up." He squinted and looked around the room. Mrs. Bassett was standing by the bedroom door; her daughter was with her. The two boys were in the kitchen, carrying rifles.

"This is Abe and Sam," the old man said by way of introduction.

Heinz nodded and spoke to the women. "Take blankets and warm coats and some water and head out onto the prairie. There are plenty of draws and gullies out there to hide in. Walk at least an hour, say two and a half miles before stopping. Don't come in until dawn, and then be careful."

Bassett said, "Marshal, I don't think it's safe for them to be out there."

"Safer there than here," Joe Leslie said.

"And I won't be worrying about them out there," Heinz said. "Ladies, would you please get your things right away?"

Joe Leslie helped them and Ed came in. Heinz said, "Bring in the rifles and ammunition." He turned to Oliver Bassett and the two boys. "I want to set up a good cross fire to pin down anyone that comes in the yard. What kind of roof do you have?"

"Sod."

"And how far is it to water?"

"Out the back door. Fifteen yards to the well."

"Root cellar?"

"Yes, but you got to get to it from outside."

Heinz frowned. "I noticed as I rode in that the corral half circles the place." Ed Leslie came back inside with the Henry repeaters and ammunition and passed the rifles around. "Ed, I want you and one of the Bassett boys to take a position at the far end of the corral. See what you can find there for cover."

"Right," Ed said. He winked at the oldest boy. "Come on, button. You can admire that shootin' iron when it's daylight."

They went out and Heinz said, "Bassett, you and your other son get into the loft of the barn. Joe and I will stay in the house. Don't open fire until I begin shooting."

Bassett nodded. "Somebody better tell that other fella that."

"He already knows it," Heinz said. "Get over to the barn and be quiet."

They went out and he closed the door and shot the bolt, then went through the house to check the back door. He came back and found Joe Leslie nosing around. Leslie said, "We can make a good fight of it here."

"Yes, I think so." He went to each window and drew the muslin curtains closed so that the light would be visible but anyone outside would have difficulty identifying those in the house. He looked at his watch. "We might as well make a pot of coffee. I don't expect them until late."

Joe Leslie went over to the stove and poked up the fire and pushed the coffee pot to the center. Carl Heinz said, "This may be the night when the police are through in Texas. If we get Dane, it may turn a suspicious eye on the whole sorry mess. Once Dane is in custody, I want every eastern newspaper to get this story. It's not the military commanders who have to be convinced. It's the politicians in Washington."

"Providin' we don't get the hell shot out of us," Leslie said. He tended the coffee pot until it began to boil, then filled two cups and took one to Heinz. "It's liable to be a hot night before we see dawn." He hunkered down, back to the wall. "Ever been licked good, Carl?"

"No," Heinz said, "but I suppose it's long overdue." He blew on his coffee and sipped it. "I suppose we were fools, the three of us, for coming out here without more men. But to me it's important to lick Dane on a personal basis."

"He might not show."

"He'll show," Heinz said, "because this is his kind of a fight. Get some sleep."

"Toss you for it," Leslie said and flipped a coin.

"Heads," Heinz said and watched it come up. He laughed and stretched out.

Joe Leslie said, "That'll teach me not to be fair."

Heinz could not think of this as sleep. Rest, yes, but not sleep, not with the ear listening and the eyes ready to fly open, not with his mind alert; sleep was tranquil, an opiate; this was merely motionless waiting.

He heard the sound just as Leslie touched him on the shoulder.

The lamps were down and he knew that Leslie must have turned them down and it irritated him to know this had happened and he had not been aware of it. He went to the window, raised up and peered out and for a moment he could see nothing. Then he made out the shape of the riders in the yard; he could count eight and he knew there were more.

They were spaced yards apart, halfway between the house and the barn and there was no way for Heinz to make out Dane, or anyone in command.

Then Dane yelled, "You in the house! Wake up in there!"

Heinz placed the voice, somewhere near the middle of the yard. Joe Leslie glanced at him and Heinz deepened his voice and yelled, "Who is it? What you want?"

"This is the police," Dane said. "Come out. I want to talk to you."

"I ain't done nothin'," Heinz said heavily. "It's late. Camp the night and we'll talk in the mornin'."

"We'll talk now," Dane said. "Do we have to come in after you?"

"If you're that set on it," Heinz yelled, "then come ahead."

He heard Dane giving orders and they risked a look over the sill of the window and saw two of the policemen wheel their horses, ride to the corral and lift off the top pole. They put ropes to it and two more sided them and they kicked their horses into a run, heading for the house.

"Watch for splinters," Leslie said and ducked down.

With the pole slung between them, they made for the door and at the last minute they wheeled away, casting the pole like a huge spear.

The door came off the hinges and was carried clean to the opposite wall and the dust and din had hardly settled when three policemen burst in, guns drawn. The first in got three steps past the threshold and he died there and the two following him were bullet-hit in the doorway; one managed to turn and make it partially off the porch before falling.

Dane gave the order to fire but this was drowned

out by the cross fire coming from the barn and corral. He was taken by surprise, caught between three enemies, and his men almost bolted. Several fell off their horses.

Heinz said, "Keep shooting." He made it to the door and ducked out before Joe Leslie could stop him or Dane's men could bring a gun to bear on him. He ran off the porch and around the corner of the house and two shots tried to reach him but they were both tardy. Heinz skirted the house at a run, came around the other side and found that he was within twenty yards of reaching Paul Dane. The trouble was, so much lead was flying around that a man didn't stand much chance of making it; Ed Leslie and the Bassetts were doing plenty of shooting, thinning out Dane's troopers and keeping them boxed in the yard.

Only a fool would chance a run across the yard, Heinz thought and began to sprint. He lost his hat and he thought a stray bullet ticked him but he didn't stop to find out. When he reached Dane, he swung his rifle like a club and mauled the man off the horse. Then he jumped him, pinning him down, and when Dane started to fight, Heinz shoved the muzzle of the rifle under his chin and said, "Call them off or I'll blow your brains all over the yard."

It would have been a messy way to die and Dane didn't think much of dying in the first place. He yelled, "Cease fire! Cease fire!"

"Tell them to drop their guns," Heinz said and when Dane hesitated he shoved a little harder with the rifle.

"Put up your weapons! Holster your weapons!"

Heinz got off Dane and pulled him to his feet. Joe Leslie came from the house with a bright lantern and Ed and the Bassetts appeared, covering the three men Dane had left. One of the Bassett boys limped, having been hit in the calf of the leg; no one else seemed to be hurt.

The old man fetched another lantern and held it high. Ed Leslie took Dane's pistol from his hand and sniffed it, then threw it on the ground.

"Never been fired," he said.

Dane was regaining his composure. "I'll charge you all with murder for this."

"Let's see your warrant for the arrest of Bassett and his sons," Heinz asked.

"It's in my office," Dane said.

"You're a liar," Heinz snapped. "There never was a warrant for them. Dane, I've got you cold this time. This was supposed to go like the Slade killings, wasn't it?"

"You're insane."

Heinz wasn't going to argue about it; he had his man and he was ready to take it to court. He motioned to the Leslies. "Tie them, get them mounted. We'll leave for town in fifteen minutes." He turned to the Bassett boy. "Are you hit bad?"

"Naw, it's nothin'," he said.

160

"I hate to put this on you, Bassett, but if you and your sons could tend to the burying—"

"Glad to do it, marshal," the old man said.

"Mark the graves carefully and hold all identification for me," Heinz said. "And you'd better take care of that leg, son."

"I will. They sure wrecked the hell out of the door, didn't they?" He turned away and limped into the cabin, followed by his father and brother.

Dane stood under arrest; he seemed to have given up any idea of bolting. The Leslies were getting the surviving policemen mounted and they brought Dane's horse over. "Get on it," Heinz said.

"With my hands tied behind me?"

"Get on it or I'll put you across it."

Dane managed to get on and when his horse was brought up, Heinz swung up, riding just behind Dane. He headed out while the Leslies brought up the rear with the other prisoners. For a time, no one spoke, then Heinz said, "Expensive night, huh, captain? You start out with twelve men and now there's only four. I'll bet you told the troopers it would be a cakewalk, just an old man and his sons." He laughed. "We put the women out on the prairie. Bassett will send one of his boys after them."

"He came to you," Dane said.

"Yep," Heinz said. "You thought he was too scared to talk, didn't you?"

161

"I have nothing to say until I have a chance to discuss this with a legal officer," Dane said. "No admissions, Heinz. Nothing at all except this trumped up charge."

"We're going to let Colonel Shannon decide how trumped up it is."

Dane turned his head, then laughed. "If you're putting any hope in Shannon then I'm as good as free. You're not a very smart politician, Heinz. Put yourself in Shannon's place. What can he really do to me without hurting himself? If he hangs me he'll threaten to expose a little bit of rottenness all over Texas. He may even convince some people in Washington that the Negro police policy is a failure and they'll disband the force. So what? All Shannon will get out of it is a miserable post somewhere and no more chance for promotion. Sure, he's a hero for cleaning up the mess, but back in Washington he'll be the man who made a lot of faces red. You don't get ahead in the army by proving your superiors were wrong." He dropped back until he almost sided Heinz. "You know what he'll do? He'll throw me out at the worst. But I expect him to dismiss the charges. And when he does that, make tracks fast because there won't be a horse so fast I can't catch it, or a hole small enough for you to hide."

"Got it all figured out, huh?"

"To the letter. Shannon's been stringing you

along, Heinz. What could he do but pat you on the back and tell you to go ahead, but all along he's been hoping you'd fall on your face because nothing could be worse for him than to have you succeed."

"I'd make you a bet on that," Heinz said.

"You've already made it," Dane said. "Your life if I'm right."

"And yours if *I'm* right," Heinz said.

"No, I don't think so. Like it or not—and how I got the rank doesn't matter—I'm still an officer in the army and they won't hang me. You're the only man who can lose, Heinz, for dismissed charges or dismissed from service, I'll come for you."

"Where are you going to get the nerve?"

Dane laughed. "Does it take that? Can a man watch his back all the time? Sleep with his eyes open? No, you've got to let down and when you do, I'll put my bullet right into your back."

"I should have let Wes Hardin draw on you that time," Heinz said.

"That was a mistake, wasn't it? But then, you gallant bastards always make mistakes like that."

"You're counting an awful lot on Colonel Shannon's reluctance to put his career on the block," Heinz said. "He's more man than you think. I wouldn't want my chances to be hanging so slim."

"Do you see worry on my face?" Dane asked. "Heinz, you got out too early. You should be fifty-five and a major and praying you'd make light colonel before retirement at half pay. My father was like that. To hell with everyone until then, but he changed, turned into a whining boot licking shadow of a man. And he never made it, Heinz. He went out a major. All that hand-kissing for nothing. I hated him for being that way, hated him for changing, hated him for being someone that had to change."

"Is he alive today?"

"No."

"Then you've got something to be grateful for." Dane frowned. "Why do you say that?"

"You'd make him sick," Heinz said and prodded him with the rifle. "Keep riding a little farther ahead. You smell bad."

16

Caleb Early, after concluding an enjoyable evening with Cecilia Pritchard, got into his buggy and made the long drive back to town. He wasn't happy about this for the night was chilly and there were more than a few miles ahead of him, but he thought this necessary, to arrive in town in early morning so that people could see it. They had seen him leave, and the Pritchards, like it or not, would have to admit that he spent the evening there, and any fool who could add two and two could figure that he wouldn't have had time to ride clear out to Bassett's place.

Caleb Early wanted no doubt in anyone's mind that he had no part of the trouble at Bassett's.

He would like to have stopped awhile and slept, but he kept on driving, timing his pace and the remaining miles carefully, and arrived at the hotel shortly after sunup. There was a normal air to the town; merchants swept their walks and put out barrels of goods on display, and Early thought about this, figuring that perhaps no one knew about the trouble. It might be too early, he thought and went to his room and slept.

When he woke the sun was slanting and he had the room clerk bring him something to drink, and a sandwich from the kitchen and after he had relocked the door, Early sat down by the small table and got out pencil and paper. He had his story ready, and now he was about to put the capstone on it, a bill of sale for Bassett's cattle. It hadn't been hard to steal one of the chits Bassett had signed at the store and from this, Early carefully traced the man's name, then filled out the bill of sale and put it in his pocket.

All he'd have to do now would be to go to the store, order some cigars or something, and drop the chit behind the counter. The owner would find it and blame himself for being careless.

Planning, Early thought, slipping into his coat, is everything. You just can't plan too carefully.

165

Carl Heinz had taken care not to draw attention to Dane's arrest; they returned late, locked the prisoners in cells, and went down to the office. Dawn was yet two hours away and they brewed some coffee and drank it and finally Heinz said, "I've got to see Pete Burgess."

Joe Leslie looked up. "At this hour?"

"Any hour," Heinz said and went out.

He walked to the edge of town to the police barracks and found it dark and abandoned. Then he turned and went back, cutting into the alley behind the saloon, and knocked lightly on the door. He heard a movement, then Pete Burgess said, "Who the hell is it?"

"Heinz."

The bolt shot back and the door opened and Heinz stepped inside. Burgess put a match to a lamp, then he smiled widely. "Under the manure pile, now there's a place for a grave," he said.

Heinz drew his breath in sharply. "You found him?"

Burgess nodded. "We tore up every plank in the barracks and dug up half the yard before we found him. It's the sergeant all right. They buried his saddle and gear with him, I suppose so there wouldn't be any trace. Likely they killed his horse somewhere on the prairie and left it to the coyotes and wolves."

"I went to the barracks," Heinz said. "Where are the rest of Dane's police?"

"Locked in the stable and under guard," Burgess explained. "They're kind of scared, Carl, but I don't think any of 'em know anything or they'd have talked." He looked at the bullet rent on the coat sleeve, and the hole through the crown of the hat. "Looks like you had an excitin' night. You do any good out there?"

"Yes," Heinz said. "Have you seen any sign of the army?"

"No. They supposed to be around?"

Heinz nodded. "Where's Early?"

"Courtin' the Pritchard girl, I hear. Don't believe it though."

"Cecilia?"

"That's what I hear," Burgess said.

"Somehow that doesn't figure," Heinz said, then shrugged. "I'm going to catch a little sleep." He turned to the door then stopped. "What have you done with the sergeant?"

"We covered him back up," Burgess said. "You know, he's been dead for some time and—"

Heinz waved his hand. "Yes, I know. We've got Dane and three others in jail. Keep it under your hat."

"I didn't hear a thing," Burgess said and let him out.

Walking back to the jail, Heinz thought about Cecilia and Caleb Early and it just didn't add up; she was too proud to keep company with a man like Early and Heinz didn't for a moment

167

believe that Cecilia was blind to what Early was.

He suspected that the general had something to do with this; they were playing a game, that was his conclusion as he went into his outer office. The two Leslie boys were stretched out on bunks in the side room but they were not asleep. After Heinz locked the door and sat down to take off his boots, Ed Leslie said, "Pete have any luck?"

"The best. Early's got an alibi. He was out to the Pritchard place." He settled back and sighed and put his hands behind his head. "You know, Ed, in my military career I had a lot of chances to make some bad mistakes, and every time I had that chance, I'd get a little indigestion and it would warn me to back off and think it over. Now there wasn't any reason to try and kill the Bassetts except for those cattle, and once they're dead, Early just can't go out there and take them; he knows he couldn't get away with that. So what's he going to do?"

"If he could have bought 'em, there wouldn't be any need to kill anybody," Ed said softly. "Bassett would have to give him a bill of sale in any case. In Texas you don't put a rope on another man's brand without a bill of sale or written authorization. Why, when Nix and Owen drove north, they had papers for every critter, and a trail brand to boot."

"Exactly," Heinz said. "Now if it gets out that Dane's raid fizzled, Early will pull in his horns and wait another chance. But if word gets out that the Bassetts are dead, killed like the Slades, we may just flush our bird, Early, into fluttering his wings."

"By God, it might work," Ed said, raising on an elbow. "No one comes near the jail; they wouldn't know we got Dane in a cell. And he could yell his head off and no one would pay any attention. But Bassett may come into town and—" He swung his feet to the floor and pulled on his boots. "I'll saddle a fresh horse and start back."

"If you run into Lieutenant Provine and his company, shoo him on into town, but tell him what we're up to. I want those troopers to spread the word in the saloon and up and down the street."

"Will do," Ed said and put on his pistol belt.

Heinz let him out and went back to the bunk and found Joe Leslie awake. "You heard?"

"Yep," Joe said, grinning. "I lost my shut eye earlier. This time I'm keepin' it." He rolled over, bumped his hips against the mattress and sighed contentedly.

Heinz woke before nine o'clock and nudged Joe Leslie awake. Food for the prisoners had to be ordered, and while Joe went down the street to get it, Heinz went up the stairs to the cell blocks.

Wes Hardin was stretched out on his bunk; Dane and his police troopers were farther down, and as Heinz passed, Hardin said, "I see you got him. He goin' to hang?"

169

"That's for the military governor to decide," Heinz said.

Hardin laughed. "I guess it's a foolish wish then."

"Between the two of you," Heinz said, "his chances of stretching a rope are better than yours."

He walked on and looked into Dane's cell and found the man sitting on the cot, staring at the wall. Heinz checked the other prisoners, including the two new ones the Leslie boys had brought back just before going to the Bassett place, then he went on down the stairs to the front office.

When the food came, Heinz had them put it on the desk; he allowed no one in the cell blocks except deputies, and they always went unarmed for he didn't want to run the risk of a prisoner grabbing a gun. Joe took the trays upstairs and he made several trips, then he came in and sat down.

"Those two gunfighters are in a sour frame of mind," he said.

"Nothing to be done about it," Heinz said. "Has Dane seen them yet?"

Joe Leslie shook his head. "I don't think he'd recognize 'em anyway." He laughed. "If Dane had only known the day he came in here with that damned story about the—"

"He didn't know," Heinz said. "And that's what gets a man in the sweat of it, Joe, what he doesn't know."

It was nearly noon when Lieutenant Provine

and his company came into town and Provine stopped at the jail and had the sergeant dismiss the men. He came in and shook hands with Heinz. Provine was a young, slender man, tough as a musket sling, and as sharp as a good skinning knife. He sat down and took one of Heinz's cigars, then said, "We ran into your deputy nearly four hours ago. My men will dutifully spread the word, complete with the gory details. There were no survivors, so there won't be any conflicting stories." He puffed his cigar and looked carefully at Heinz. "A little strategy, Carl?"

"I hope so," Heinz said. He got up. "Can I buy you a drink?"

"How can I turn it down?" Provine asked and they went down the street together. "I understand that the colonel will arrive day after tomorrow with his entourage to hold court."

"That's the schedule," Heinz said and pressed open the door to Burgess' place. Already he could detect a new excitement in the talk and men were going in and out because they had some new and terrible news to spread.

At the bar, Burgess served them. He looked at Heinz and said, "Terrible about the Bassett family, wasn't it?"

"Very bad," Heinz said. He glanced around to see if anyone was in attentive earshot, then in a softer voice, said, "Water the drinks and keep them coming."

171

Burgess nodded and moved on to new customers down the bar, and they stood there for better than an hour, drinking the stuff Burgess kept sliding in front of them. No one noticed them, and the cut whiskey had no effect on them, but it gave them an excuse to be there, and Heinz needed that.

The word would get to Early, and it was just a matter of waiting, and by two o'clock Heinz was beginning to get impatient. He made an effort to push this aside, and finally he and Provine went to a table to sit.

A little after four, Caleb Early came in, went to the bar for a rye whiskey, then saw Heinz and the lieutenant and moved through the crowd to their table.

"May I sit down?" Early asked.

Heinz toed a chair away from the table and waited. Early bit the end off a cigar and got it going, then finished his second drink.

"I just heard the news," he said. "I was driving all night from the Pritchard place and slept late. Terrible. Those murderers will have to be caught, marshal."

"I've got a deputy out there now looking around," Heinz said. "You were at Pritchard's place?"

"Yes," Early said, smiling. "Miss Cecilia and I are keeping company. I got there in the early afternoon and left shortly after ten last night."

"I see," Heinz said. "Of course, the next time I see the general, you won't mind my asking him, will you?"

"Not at all," Early said. "But this horrible affair puts me in an awkward position."

"How's that?"

"Why, because I bought Bassett's cattle not three days ago," Early said. "I have his bill of sale, but I expect it will take the authority of your office and a command from Colonel Shannon to give me possession of the cattle."

"You wouldn't mind letting me see that bill of sale, would you?"

"Not at all," Early said. "I came over to talk to you about that very thing." He glanced at Lieutenant Provine. "If you wish to keep the bill of sale for a few days, the lieutenant here can witness your receipt. That paper represents a lot of money and nearly fourteen hundred head of cattle to me."

"You haven't shown it to me yet," Heinz said.

Early laughed and took it out of his pocket. Heinz looked at it, then dropped his hand casually to his lap. When it came back in sight it held a cocked .44 Remington and it pointed at the center of Caleb Early's breastbone.

"You're under arrest," Heinz said.

"Wha—why, of all the ridiculous—" His face flushed and he calmed himself with an effort. "What the hell's the idea?"

"Bassett never signed this bill of sale," Heinz said.

"The devil he didn't!"

"The devil he did," Heinz said. He smiled thinly. "Early, let me tell you something. It'll be a shock, so brace yourself. None of the Bassetts are dead. The raid never came off because I and two deputies laid an ambush for Paul Dane. He lost eight men and I've got three troopers and Dane in a cell right now."

The blood seemed to drain from Early's face and his knuckles were white as he gripped the edge of the table. "That's a lie!" He looked at Phillip Provine, who was gently shaking his head from side to side.

"It's no lie," Provine said. "You've been suckered, Early."

None of this talk had been loud, but the smell of trouble passed through this crowd and silenced them; they stood in rows, watching.

Early's breathing was a deep sawing, and he stared at Carl Heinz and knew then how deeply he had been pulled in. With a lunge he went against the table and both Provine and Heinz were knocked backward in their chairs and spilled onto the sawdust.

Heinz rolled away as Early drew his gun and fired, the heavy bullet raking a splinter off the edge of the table. He was backing toward the door, earing back the hammer for another shot when Heinz brought his .44 up and dropped the hammer. The bullet spun Early and he staggered and caught himself and fired again, but Heinz had rolled away. He lay prone on the floor, arm outstretched, took his sight, and dropped Early with a shot in the left breast.

Then he got to his feet, as did Provine, and they walked over to the man and turned him over. Burgess came from around the bar and said, "Well, he had guts enough to make a fight of it anyway."

"He was a desperate man," Provine said, and motioned for the sergeant to step over. "Get four men and carry him into the back room." He reholstered his pistol and looked at Heinz. "If that's what it takes to enforce the law, I'll stick to soldiering. These point blank gunfights are not for me."

"I didn't want it to end this way," Heinz said regretfully. "I could have made a deal with him, got him off light if he'd helped convict Dane. Now I'll have to do it the hard way."

17

Carl Heinz expected a certain influx of the military for the trials, but he had no idea he'd draw so much attention; Shannon arrived with his staff of officers, fourteen of them, and two troops of cavalry to set up housekeeping at the edge of town. From east Texas, Colonel Crisp brought one troop and six officers, and before the day finished, three more commanders arrived with their retinue and there wasn't a room in the hotel to be had.

And Texans for miles around migrated to the town, living in rough camps and in wagons and in the loft of the stable and any other vacant space they could find.

Colonel Shannon called a conference and he used the street floor of the hotel for this; so many officers attended that even this lobby was none too large.

Charges against the prisoners in custody were registered and the officiating officers were appointed, Shannon presiding, with Colonel Crisp and Colonel Brackett siding him. The prisoners were to be represented by legal officers, appointed by the court since there were no civilian attorneys to represent them. Lieutenant Provine acted as prosecutor for the people, and at his suggestion, General Pritchard was appointed to act as defense counsel for the civilian prisoners and a rider was dispatched to the general's home to bring him to town.

The order of arraignment had not yet been established and Heinz spent most of three days with the legal officers, helping them shape their arguments. Lieutenant Provine, who would face these men in court, continually stood at Heinz's elbow to make sure that the defense counsel learned only the facts in relation to the charges.

Pritchard and his family arrived and a place was found for them in a private home and Heinz hoped to get away and see Nan, but he just couldn't pry free enough time, for it was always late at night before he was finished.

Three days of this finished it; Provine was ready with his witnesses and the legal officers defending the prisoners were ready and Heinz, leaving the Leslies in charge, walked to one of the quiet back streets where the Pritchards stayed. Although it was after ten o'clock, the general and his sons sat on the porch, smoking their cigars and when Heinz came up they shook hands and offered him a chair.

"You've been a stranger," Nathan Pritchard said, smiling.

"I feel like a hound dog that's about run out," Heinz said. "Right now I could use ten days to go fishing."

Nix Pritchard laughed. "I've got a sister who's already thought of a better way to spend ten days, Carl." He got up. "She went to bed early but I'll tell her you're here." He stepped inside and the general elevated his feet to the porch railing.

"Carl," he said, "whose case is going to be heard first in the mornin'?"

"I couldn't say, sir. As a marshal, people don't tell me much."

"I'm defending Hardin and the two gunfighters," Pritchard said. "Frankly, suh, I'm in one hell of a squeeze. They've all killed Negro police. Killed Texans too. I don't see how that can be denied. Unless I want 'em hung, I'll have to prove provocation, some semblance of justification. That's not as simple as it sounds."

"Frankly, I don't think it can be done," Heinz said. "Hardin is the only one of the three I really know, and he's just plain killer now. All the reasons he thought he had are gone. He shoots because it's the first thing he thinks of." He looked up as Nix came back out.

"They got a nice parlor," Nix said, sitting down.

"Thanks," Heinz said and went inside.

The place belonged to a merchant who was staying with a married sister while the general was in town and although there was no reflected, immediate wealth, the house was well appointed, speaking of the prosperous days before the war. Heinz walked up and down a bit, then he heard a light step on the stairs and Nan came in, a dressing gown belted about her. They came to each other and kissed and he held her without saying anything, then they sat down on the sofa and he held her hands.

"Shall I offer excuses or keep my mouth shut?" he asked.

"Carl, I do understand. But when does it end?"

"The job or you living one place and me another?"

"I'm too sensible to ask you to give up the job," she said. "I want you to have a house built. Pick a spot with trees."

"Why don't you pick it while you're here?" he asked.

"I'm going to accept that as a genuine offer," she said and leaned forward and kissed him briefly. "As a matter of fact, I saw a place that suits me just fine. I even found out who owns the land." She began to block out the house with her hands. "I like adobe because it's cool in the summer and snug in the winter. Something built around a court with the trees and well enclosed. It shouldn't cost you more than three thousand dollars. Is that too much?"

He smiled and blew out a breath of mock relief. "I'll take that before the price goes up." He glanced at the wall clock ticking over the fireplace. "I may not get a chance to see you in court, or talk to you. But I'll see about dinner tomorrow night at the hotel."

"You could come here."

He shook his head. "Just you and I alone."

"I like that," she said, smiling.

He kissed her again and went out and when he stepped off the porch, Owen Pritchard said, "That was short."

"Never overdo a good thing," Heinz said.

When he got back to his office, he found Ed on duty; Joe was in his bunk sleeping. Heinz took off his pistol belt and hung it up, then his shirt and washed his hands and face at the sideboard.

"People stopped comin' in and out," Ed said with relief. "I feel kind of sorry for Lieutenant Jackson. He's got to defend Dane and he don't like it none."

"I think I know him. A short, blond man?" Heinz nodded. "He'll give Dane more of a break than he deserves."

He walked into the other room and sat down on a bunk. Ed Leslie turned the lamp down in the outer office and came in, leaving the door open. He laid his pistols on a stand near his bed and stretched out. "Tomorrow," he said, "I thought Joe and I would station ourselves in the back of the room near the door. They're going to hold this in the hotel lobby, ain't they?"

"Yes," Heinz said and took off his boots; he sat there rubbing the soles of his feet. "Carry repeaters; a pistol might be too handy for someone to grab if there's trouble. And you can always use a rifle as a club if you have to. We want to keep down the possibility of anyone getting hurt by a wild shot." He laid back and pulled a blanket over him. "If I'm not up by sunup, boot me out."

"Who's gonna boot me?" Ed Leslie asked and blew out the lamp.

The crowd was such that Colonel Shannon had soldiers on friendly guard duty along the street;

the hotel lobby was packed and tables had been arranged for the three judges, the defense counsel, and the prosecutor.

At nine o'clock, the court was brought into session and Shannon's aide read the government order authorizing the proceedings. Immediately afterward, General Nathan Pritchard rose and addressed the court.

"Gentlemen, may I inquire as to which indictment will be read first?"

"The outlaw, Wesley Hardin," Shannon said.

"Then I respectfully petition the court to withhold the indictment until after Captain Dane has been tried," Pritchard said.

Colonel Brackett said, "Before the court can entertain such a petition, it would have to have substantial reason." He was a small, dry-mannered man with dark eyes and the habit of squinting them when he talked.

"In the interests of justice and the defense of the prisoners," Pritchard said, "much depends upon the degree of guilt or innocence of Captain Dane. I can not introduce as evidence or discussion facts that have not been established. It is through the trial of Captain Dane that these facts, or the lack of them will be established."

Colonel Crisp said, "I see no reason why this request cannot be granted." He looked at the others. "After all, we're here to serve justice, not see how many we can hang."

There was a murmured discussion, then Shannon said, "Granted, general. Mr. Provine, you may read the indictment against Captain Dane. Marshal Heinz, will you have the prisoner brought to this courtroom."

Heinz turned and motioned to the Leslies, who went out and he stood there and listened to Provine read the charges, and it made him feel good to know that he really had Dane deeply stuck in the mud. He kept watching Shannon's expression, and Brackett's, and found them frowning for this was bad trouble for a man who wore a uniform and a military title and the stain of it would touch them and Heinz had the troubled feeling that perhaps Dane was partially right; they would have to paint him white to clean themselves.

Paul Dane was brought in and seated, and then it was Provine's show; he called Carl Heinz to the stand and he was sworn in.

He had Heinz relate to the court the circumstances of his visit to the Slade place, and what he had found when he got there; Provine interrupted often to bring out small details as though he wanted nothing, however slight, to be left out. Clearly, from the clues, the court could draw the conclusion that Heinz had drawn, that the murdered man had inflicted a wound on one of the assailants before dying.

"Now," Provine said, "after finding evidence

182

that a wounded man had been taken away, did you conduct a search for him?"

"Well, yes, although I wasn't marshal at the time," Heinz said. "All indications led me to believe that the wounded man was Captain Dane's sergeant, Jerico Frank."

"Object!" Jackson shouted. "There is equal indication that Sergeant Frank has deserted his duty. I move that the marshal has expressed an opinion and ask that it be stricken."

"So ordered," Shannon said. He looked at Heinz. "Stick to the facts."

"I have no further questions to ask at this time," Provine said, "although I would like to recall the witness."

"You may step down," Shannon said.

"Call Pete Burgess to the stand."

Burgess was seated and sworn and Provine leaned on the arm of the chair. "You're in the saloon business?"

"Cattle too."

"How is business?"

"Good, now that cattle are being driven north," Burgess said.

Provine smiled. "I understand that you're good with a shovel."

"I know how to dig," Burgess said.

Jackson got up. "Really, does this have *any* point?"

"Sit down," Colonel Shannon said. "Go on, Mr. Provine, but don't take all day."

"Yes, sir. Now, Mr. Burgess, a few days ago you and some men did considerable digging. Is that so?" Burgess nodded. "Who ordered you to dig?"

"The marshal."

"Did he tell you where to dig?"

"Yeah, he said to dig up the yard around the police barracks. We did."

"And what did you find?"

"Sergeant Frank buried under the manure pile."

"Hah!" Provine said, jubilant. "So he didn't go off somewhere and desert?"

"I object," Jackson said. "Gentlemen, what are you trying to establish? We will concede that the sergeant is dead and that we were mistaken in assuming that he deserted. However, no connection can be drawn between this event and the accused."

"Your objection is well taken," Shannon said. "Do you have any further questions, Mr. Provine?"

"Just one, sir." He looked at Burgess. "Could you tell what the sergeant died of?"

"A bullet in the gut," Burgess said.

"Thank you," Provine said. "You may step down." He looked at Heinz. "I would like to recall Marshal Heinz to the stand."

Burgess got up and Heinz sat down. Shannon said, "You are still under oath. Carry on, Mr. Provine."

"Thank you. Marshal, relate to the court the circumstances of Mr. Bassett's visit to your office."

Heinz went through it, but Provine questioned him on a few points. "He clearly indicated that the killings at the Slade place were being used as a threat?"

"Early visited him twice. The last time he mentioned that it was a terrible thing, what had happened to the Slades, and that it could happen to other stubborn men."

Jackson popped erect. "Gentlemen, a dead man said these things. What does it have to do with the accused?"

Shannon said, "Mr. Provine, I suggest you stick closer to the point."

"Yes, sir. Let's go on, marshal. Later Captain Dane came to you and told you he had found an outlaw camp some miles from town. Is that so?"

"Yes, he described the men, both wanted criminals."

"And you told him you'd look into it?"

"Yes, I said that. But he was lying. He hadn't seen those men at all."

"Objection," Jackson said, bouncing up. "Gentlemen, how long must we suffer through this man's opinions? Clearly he's hostile toward the accused and had no foundation, other than his personal feelings, for drawing such a conclusion."

"Well?" Shannon asked.

Carl Heinz smiled. "The gunfighters, Ben Bickerstaff and Lee of Texas had already been arrested by deputies Joe and Ed Leslie and were sleeping in cells upstairs at the precise moment Paul Dane stood there spouting his damned lies. Now object to that if you can."

A tossed skunk couldn't have caused more of an uproar and Shannon pounded long for order and when he got it he said, "The court will recess for thirty minutes. Marshal, I'd like to see you in one of the rooms."

18

Colonel Shannon used the hotel office for the meeting, and Colonel Crisp and Brackett were there, as well as Lieutenant Provine and Carl Heinz. Shannon leaned against the wall, his brows wrinkled; for a moment he said nothing and they all waited.

Finally he said, "Carl, you want the rope for Dane, don't you?"

"That's right," Heinz said.

Shannon looked at Lieutenant Provine. "How much can you prove? I mean, prove beyond a doubt?"

"I can put a Negro policeman on the stand, sir, who was at the Slade place the night they were all killed. He was also at Bassett's place when the attempt was made there. If that doesn't convince the court—"

Shannon waved his hand. "Hell, we're convinced,

but let's consider this a moment. There are good police and there are bad, but we're painting them all black here. We want Dane out, but we can do it without undermining the entire program."

"The program's no good," Heinz said. "It's about time some people in Washington found that out. Colonel, when I was bringing Dane back in, he told me he'd never hang."

A hardness came into Shannon's eyes. "Did he tell you why?"

"Yes, he said you thought too much of your career to throw it away by angering your superiors." Heinz smiled thinly. "It seems that he knew you better than I did."

"I am after a compromise," Shannon said. "Not a deal, Carl, but a just, reasonable compromise."

Colonel Brackett cleared his throat. "Marshal, the court would like to see Captain Dane change his plea from innocent to guilty to a lesser charge."

"What charge?" Heinz asked.

Crisp said, "The point is to remove Captain Dane, isn't it? Dismiss him dishonorably. Perhaps even some time in prison."

"What charge?" Heinz repeated.

Shannon said, "You're stubborn. All right, what about misconduct in office?"

"Try again," Heinz said.

Brackett said, "Attempted murder?"

"What about Hardin and Bickerstaff and Lee of Texas?" Provine asked.

187

Shannon frowned. "I don't understand. They'll be tried." He grew impatient. "Gentlemen, look now, I don't have to haggle. I can make the deal with Lieutenant. Jackson. I'm not in disagreement with what you want, Carl. The police have to go, but let us do it our way."

"You're mistaken," Heinz said. "You make the deal with me. We've got the evidence and nothing can stop us from presenting it. If you want to make a deal, you'll have to make it with me and Lieutenant Provine."

Crisp said, "What is it then?"

"Dismiss the charges against the civilian prisoners."

"And?" Shannon said.

"And Dane can plead guilty to attempted murder and be sentenced to dismissal from the service."

"No!" Provine said quickly, forgetting that he was putting his career in danger. "Carl, I never thought you'd make a deal like that. Well you go ahead, but I'm out to make the charge of murder stick."

"You'll never make it," Heinz said. "Can't you see that?"

"Yes, but by God, I'll still try."

"Do it my way," Heinz said. "Dane swears he'll kill me so let him have his chance. I can do what the court hasn't guts enough to do." He looked at the three officers. "I can say that because I'm not in the army."

"If you kill him it won't mean anything," Provine said quickly. "He's got to be taken by the court, punished by the court." He let his glance touch all three men. "All of you have enjoyed distinguished military careers. I want you to ask yourselves whether or not you would like to see this decision on your records."

"You're getting out of line," Colonel Brackett said.

"Yes, sir," Provine said. "We all are, aren't we, sir?"

Brackett cleared his throat. "It's been a long time since a first lieutenant had to remind me what was right. I'm not afraid of Washington. Damn it, when you come right down to it, the opinion of the people is on our side. Even Washington can't buck that." He looked at Crisp. "I go for no deal. What about you, Ralph?"

"I haven't crusaded since I was a lieutenant and was knocked down on the promotion list for it." He sighed. "Shannon?"

"Two against one, huh? I'm a fool."

"Mitch, let's present a solid front to these people," Crisp said. "It'll be harder to crucify three colonels than two."

"All right," Shannon said. Then he looked at Heinz and smiled. "Very smart, the way you played your hand. By taking the deal you made it look cheaper than it really was."

"I made it look like it really was," Heinz said.

"Colonel, I never really believed Dane, what he said about you."

"Well, that's some comfort anyway," Shannon said. "Let's get on with this then." He opened the door and they stepped into the hotel lobby. He took his seat behind the prisoner and crossed his legs and Dane turned his head and looked at him but there was no talk, just that one look.

Lieutenant Provine paraded his witnesses, and the Bassetts testified and were cross-examined by Lieutenant Jackson, but he could make no dent in their story.

The day ended and the next began with Heinz being recalled to the stand to relate in detail the trouble at Bassett's place, and when Provine indicated that he was through, Jackson rose for his cross-examination.

"Marshal, I'd like to examine this matter of the shooting at Bassett's place. Who opened fire first?"

"We did," Heinz said. "We were barricaded inside the house when the door was broken in by Dane's men."

"And that was your reason for firing?"

"What better reason does one have to have?"

"Mr. Heinz, *I'm* asking the questions," Jackson said. "You had no reason to believe the accused was there on any but legitimate business, did you?"

"The fact that he was there at all was proof

enough that his business was not legitimate," Heinz said. "You want me to think it could be coincidence but we both know it is not."

"Object," Jackson said wearily. "I move that those remarks be stricken—"

"So moved," Shannon said. "Confine yourself to answers."

"Now," Jackson said. "On such flimsy reasoning you opened fire and in the ensuing battle, killed eight policemen in the discharge of their duty."

"Not flimsy reasons," Heinz said. "And they weren't doing their duty."

Jackson opened his mouth to object, but closed it, having changed his mind. "Marshal Heinz, I am going to ask you one more question so that you can answer it yes or no. When you arrested the accused, did he possess a weapon, a pistol or a knife or something?"

"Yes, a pistol."

"Did you examine that pistol?"

"No," Heinz said and smiled.

It shook Jackson, took him back, because it wasn't the answer he wanted or expected. Then he said, "All right then, was the pistol examined by someone else in your presence?"

"Yes," Heinz said. "My deputy, Ed Leslie examined it."

"Ah, now we're getting somewhere. Had the pistol been fired?"

191

"No," Heinz said.

"That's all, thank you." He turned away smiling and Provine stood up.

"Just a moment, marshal. I'd like to ask a few questions on re-direct, if I may." Shannon nodded and Provine came up to the witness chair. "Mr. Heinz, have you ever fought as an officer?"

"Yes."

"In what capacity?"

"Company commander and platoon commander."

Provine nodded. "When the order to cease fire was given at the Bassett place, who gave that order?"

"Captain Dane."

"As a company commander, did you give like orders?"

"Yes," Heinz said.

"Then it would be safe to assume that Captain Dane was in command of the police at Bassett's, wouldn't it?"

"Object," Jackson said, rising. "That calls for an assumption on the part of the witness and—"

"I believe," Shannon said, "that such an assumption can be safely drawn. Overruled."

"Thank you," Provine said dryly. "I was beginning to think the court would never see my point."

"There is no need for sarcasm," Shannon said. "Get on with it."

"Now, marshal, when you were in battle, giving orders, did you always fire your weapon?"

"No," Heinz said. "Generally not. The commander is too busy attending to the business of command. His weapon is largely a means of defense in case he is in personal danger."

"I see," Provine said. "And the fact that Dane's pistol was unfired did not surprise you then?"

"No, it didn't," Heinz said and Provine turned away.

"No more questions."

Shannon looked at the clock. "I believe we've had enough for today. Marshal, return the prisoner to custody. Court's adjourned until nine o'clock tomorrow morning."

The Leslie boys took Paul Dane out of the hotel and Provine came over and stood while the crowd thinned, then he said, "Carl, I'd like to sum up without bringing the Negro policeman to testify."

"Isn't that a risk?"

"Yes, but I think I can see Jackson's defense and I'd like to rest the case on what we have, let him present his defense, and then, if I have to, plead with the court to let me introduce a new witness. You see, I don't want the Negro cross-examined." He gnawed at his lip. "At best, we've made a deal with him, his freedom if he talks. Jackson just may twist that into something that will hurt our case. The Negro is a simple man; he doesn't read or write and he could be stampeded into confusing himself. Do you follow me?"

"You think the risk is too great that Jackson will make a foil of him," Heinz said.

"Yes, if you'll go along with it."

"It's your case," Heinz said. "I'm satisfied that we've got Dane."

"But not for the rope," Provine said. "Brackett and Crisp and Shannon will never hang him. It isn't in the cards, Carl."

"Yes, I guess you're right there. I want too much." He slapped Provine on the shoulder and walked down the street to his office. There was a loose-formed crowd at that end of the street and he pushed through and went inside and locked the door. Joe Leslie was coming down the stairs from the cell blocks, a jangling ring of keys in his hand.

"Our birds are in their cages," he said and hung the keys on a wall peg. "Dane wants to talk to you."

"All right," Heinz said and took off his pistol belt and laid it on the desk before going up the stairs. As he went along the hall he stopped to light the lamps; it would be dark in an hour and he thought he might save another trip this way.

Dane was sitting on his cot and he looked up when Heinz stopped at the door; he got up and came to the door and stood there with his fingers curled around the bars.

"I can see that I was wrong about Shannon," Dane said.

"That's what I told you," Heinz said. "But you have a hard time hearing things."

"I'll go on the stand tomorrow," Dane said. "I don't trust Jackson."

"He's doing all he can for you. Can't you see that?"

"It isn't enough. It's my life he's playing with." He licked his lips. "Tell Shannon I want to make a deal."

"He won't do it," Heinz said. "Take your chances, Dane. It's the best you can do."

"It isn't enough," Dane said. He made as though to turn away but it was a feint; he snaked his arm through the bars, grabbed Heinz behind the neck and pulled his face against the steel. With his free hand, Dane thrust out, sticking the sharpened point of an oak stick against Heinz's throat.

"One sound, one move," Dane said softly, "and I'll push this all the way through and you'll bleed out before you can get to the stairs." He took a deep breath. "Now call your deputy and make it natural." He pressed harder with the point. "Now do it!"

"Joe, come on up here a minute!" Heinz called.

"The keys!" Dane whispered.

"Bring the keys with you! Something's wrong with Dane!"

"Now turn a little to your left so that my hand is hidden," Dane said.

"You'll never make it," Heinz said softly.

195

Joe Leslie came up the stairs and part way down the hall, then he saw them together, the cell door between them and he stopped. "Carl?"

"Bring those keys here or I'll kill him," Dane said quickly. "I'm not fooling, Leslie." He waited and Joe came on. "Now unlock the cell door, carefully now." He pushed the door open when the lock turned and stepped into the hall, but he was still on one side and Heinz was on the other.

Joe Leslie said, "How are you going to get out of that fix?"

Dane hesitated, then he kicked out, catching Joe Leslie in the stomach, doubling him. The door swung, pushing Heinz back, crowding him between open door and the bars. Dane threw his weight against the door and banged it against Heinz's head several times, then he suddenly ran for the stairs, leaving both men stunned on the floor.

Leslie was trying to crawl after him and Heinz was shaking his head, trying to clear the ringing in his ears. He kept hoping that Ed Leslie would choose that time to come back, but it never happened.

Dane tore a rifle from the wall rack, unlocked the front door and dashed out into the street.

Joe Leslie couldn't quite stand, but Heinz staggered down the stairs, armed himself and started out when he heard the burst of shooting.

The moment he hit the street he saw the crowd

converging, and he saw the scattered meal trays where Ed Leslie had dropped them, and Dane, sprawled in the dirt, and Ed Leslie standing there, his .44 still in his hand.

Heinz rushed up and picked up the rifle Dane had taken and he sniffed the barrel, then looked at Ed Leslie. "He still didn't shoot," Heinz said and turned to get the crowd moving along.

19

Colonel Mitchell Shannon brought the court to order at nine o'clock by rapping his knuckles on the table and when quiet came, he said, "Although the accused, Captain Paul Dane, was killed while trying to escape from custody, the court would like to offer an opinion before closing the case." He glanced at Crisp and Brackett and Heinz, seated behind the defense counsel's table, knew that they had talked this over. "The accused, by his death, has removed the possibility of the court rendering a decision in this case," Shannon went on. "Still, the court feels that an opinion is justified, and perhaps even necessary for the future growth and good government of Texas. The court feels that the institution of the police, as conceived, is a failure, if not a disaster. The employment of former enslaved peoples in an administrative role, without proper training, and we feel in most cases, without proper leadership, can only lead to a situation with tragic overtones. The police, unable to cope with authority, could hardly be expected to adjudicate and enforce laws over a people who by heritage regarded them as inferior. The court does not applaud this viewpoint, but at the same time, it does not applaud governmental effort to force authority upon these people with a force intrinsically abhorrent to them."

A Texan sitting behind Heinz leaned forward and said, "What's he sayin'?"

"Never mind now," Heinz whispered. He looked at the newspapermen taking this all down. "Day after tomorrow, the eastern papers will be full of this. Be quiet and listen."

"It is the court's opinion," Shannon continued, "that the accused was not fitted for command of troops in any capacity. Had the trial continued to a conclusion, evidence points to the accused as being a man of criminal bent, a man with few redeeming qualities of leadership. All of this is beyond proof now. But the court feels that many facts have been examined and certain conclusions can be drawn that are beyond dispute. One: The concept of the Negro police force as a law enforcing agency is impractical. Two: That the personnel of this force, being largely illiterate and uninformed, easily become the tool of unscrupulous officers, whose appointments, although valid, need further and closer scrutiny by qualified military men. Three: Many crimes against this police force are in all probability falsifications, or at least distorted beyond recognizable fact." He paused and took a deep breath. "It is the court's recom-mendation that *all* units be closely examined by their respective military governors and if any irregularity exists, a recommendation for dis-missal should be instituted. Furthermore, the court recommends that the entire concept of this police unit be examined and if possible, the force dissolved and law enforcement returned to the jurisdiction of United States Marshals, or a reactivated Texas Rangers."

Heinz had not permitted firearms in the hotel lobby, and because of this there was no firing of pistols into the ceiling, but there was yelling and stamping of feet and Shannon could not bring order; he simply dismissed the court.

A bit later, Heinz was asked to come to Shannon's room and he found General Pritchard there, and Lieutenant Provine. Colonel Crisp poured the drinks, and Colonel Brackett, who had some stomach trouble, declined.

"Here," Shannon said, raising his glass, "is to a stand bravely taken, if I do say so myself."

"I'll drink to that," Heinz said. "Did you see those newspapermen from the east Texas papers? It isn't every day they get a front page story."

"About three colonels who are going to be

retired shortly?" Crisp asked. Then he laughed. "Marshal, I've been having police trouble too. So has Colonel Brackett. I've often thought how nice it would be to be rid of them."

General Pritchard swished his drink around in the glass and said, "Suhs, in view of the proceedin's, I'd like to move to have the charges dismissed against Hardin, Bickerstaff, and Lee."

"I wouldn't approve of that," Shannon said. "We haven't talked this over yet, but a change of plea is in order. Hardin's killing of that policeman can be glossed over; it would be hell to prove in the light of what's developed. But he's killed other men. He's standing trial for that."

Pritchard nodded. "Do you want him to plead guilty, suh?"

"Yes, all three of them," Shannon said. "I'll recommend a year in jail."

Pritchard gnawed his lip. "That's generous, suh. I'll do my best to convince them."

"We feel," Brackett said, "that these men are products of these turbulent times, general. Many soldiers have a difficult time adjusting to conditions after a war."

No one saw fit to mention that Hardin hadn't been a soldier, and neither had Lee of Texas, and Heinz didn't think he should mention it. He excused himself and went down to the street and through the crowd and to his office.

Joe and Ed Leslie were there and he flopped

in the chair behind his desk and leaned back. "There was a time," Heinz said, "when I wondered if Shannon had the guts to do it."

"He sure declared himself," Ed Leslie said. "And I ain't so sure it's the end of one thing and the start of another." He took out sack tobacco and rolled a cigaret. "I was talkin' to one of those newspapermen and he said in Kansas there was a whole camp of Yankee farmers fixin' to come south in search of land. We're goin' to see a lot on the trail this year, Carl. Comin' and goin' both ways."

"I expect so," Heinz said and got up. He paced restlessly about the office while both men watched him, then he turned to the door and paused with his hand on the latch. "If anyone wants me, I'm out looking at some land with trees on it."

The two men looked at each other, then Joe nodded and Heinz went out.

"He's a funny fella," Ed said.

"He don't seem funny to me," Joe said.

"Well he says funny things. You want to play some cards?"

"Why not? There's nothin' else to do around here." He got out the deck and shuffled. "You want to play casino?"

"Play anything I can beat you at," Ed Leslie said.

Joe dealt, and they played for awhile and then

201

one of the prisoners rattled the cell door and they ignored him for a time, then Ed threw down his hand and went up the stairs, the keys in his hand.

Hardin was making the racket and Ed said, "What the hell's the idea?"

"I want some fresh water," Hardin said.

"You all got fresh water this mornin'," Leslie said. "However, we aim to please our guests." He turned and picked up a fire bucket and flung the contents over Hardin, who stood dripping and cursing.

"If I wasn't locked up—"

Leslie sorted out the key, unlocked the door and flung it open. "You'd what?" he asked and stood there, unarmed, waiting. And Hardin's anger left him and he looked at Leslie and measured him and figured his chances.

Then he shrugged and said, "You've changed, Ed. I wouldn't try to take you now."

"We all change," Leslie said and relocked the door. Then he went down the stairs and sat down again. "I suppose you went through my cards and took all the good ones."

"You didn't have any good ones," Joe Leslie said. "What did Hardin want? I heard him cussing."

"He just thought he wanted somethin'," Ed said. "Play."

The house was completed in the fall and the creek ran through the walled courtyard and it was a tranquil place where he could close himself off from trouble, and there was much of that. Texas, under a carpetbag government, was a ferment of disorder, and the men she needed most, men like Shannon and Crisp and Brackett, were no longer serving her.

Dane had been right; it had cost them their careers. The federal government was turning Texas back to the Texans, but it was the northern political strings that still pulled her about, sawing her and draining her strength and giving her strength.

It was a time, Heinz thought, like war, a time a man just had to live through and hope better was coming. Personally, he was prospering; a lot of Texans were getting rich. Cattle moved north by the tens of thousands and it seemed that he couldn't make anything but money.

Shannon and Crisp stayed on, investing, along with Heinz and the Pritchards into a freighting company and a stage line from Austin to El Paso and points in between.

Ed Leslie was the marshal now; he had cut cards with Joe for the job and won, and Heinz took care of his business interests and spent more time with his wife, who was beginning to grow heavy in the early stages of her first pregnancy.

He had no intention of going into politics, but there was no avoiding it for money influence went hand in hand with political influence. Texas was split into two factions, the carpetbaggers in control, casting favors to the northern speculators, and hardcore Texans like Pritchard who lived for the day when some semblance of justice would return, when his own political party could again run Texas for Texans.

Captain Dane's trial had been a slow fuse, to Heinz's way of thinking. It spawned a year and a half of bad trouble, with many counties being placed under martial law for battles between the police and Texans became commonplace.

The police compiled a list of nearly three thousand fugitives in one hundred and eight counties and arrested and tried nearly a thousand of them before it broke, as all dams must break when the pressure is too great.

Heinz was entertaining Nathan Pritchard and Mitchell Shannon and a dozen other influential men who had traveled days to get there, and there were many meetings like this behind the walled court. There was a first snow on the ground and Cecilia was staying with them because Nan was nearing the time when she would need help, and Heinz worried about that along with other things.

It was late, after midnight, and the talk hadn't ended. Cigar butts littered the hearth and two empty whiskey bottles sat on a sideboard, along with three full ones. Pritchard said, "I'm telling you, suhs, now is the time to strike." He carried a newspaper in his hand and slapped it against his thigh. "The *Daily State Journal*, a carpetbagger's rag if there ever was one, published the story; the adjutant general has run off with thirty-four thousand dollars of public funds. I say they're turnin' against their own and when spring election comes around, it's time to play our hand."

There was a general agreement to this, and Shannon puffed on his cigar before speaking. "General, I trust you've picked out a man to run for legislator and represent us."

"That's why I called this meetin'," Pritchard said. "Gentlemen, I think we have a man who can beat the pants off the incumbent. Carl Heinz." He turned and raised his glass. "Here's to the big Yankee, and I mean that in the kindest possible sense."

He could not say afterward that they talked him into it, because he wanted to run for the office, yet their approval and support took him back a bit; they had already individually made up their minds that he was the man, and this touched him.

Yet he knew what it would mean, stumping a mighty big county, and being away from his home, and if he were elected, spending most of his time in Austin, and he didn't know how Nan would like that. But they wanted his answer and he gave it to them and then excused himself and went down a long hall to the quiet rear of the house where the bedrooms were.

Nan was awake, reading, and he closed the door

softly and sat on the edge of the bed. She put down her paper and took his hand.

"I know what they asked you," she said. "And I know what you said."

"How could you know?"

"Cecilia told me." She smiled and patted his hand. "Carl, I knew you would be more than a marshal, more even than a business man. You can't help yourself. Someday you'll be governor, if you want to be."

"I don't want to be," he said.

"You don't know now. If they need you, you'll change your mind."

"Nan, I want a good life with you."

"We'll have that," she said. Then she caught her breath and pressed a hand to her stomach. "Hasn't the doctor arrived yet? I sent Cecilia twenty minutes ago."

He stood up quickly. "Nan, you've got to wait now! I mean—" He bolted to the door. "I'll see if he's—now you wait, you hear?"

"Carl, I'm only going to have a baby."

"Only? Good Lord." He dashed off down the hall, calling for the servants, and met Cecilia and the doctor entering the hall. He was going to show him the way, but he already knew that, and Cecilia took his arm and held him back.

"It's another man's business now," she said. "It'll be all right."

"How do you know?"

"Women know, or else there wouldn't be children," she said. "Come in the kitchen and I'll fix you some coffee."

"Coffee? With my wife—"

"You'll need coffee," she said. "These things take time."

He went with her because there was nothing else to do and he sat at the table while she stoked the fire and put the pot on. "I don't want to ever lose her," he said. "Never."

She looked at him sharply, then smiled. "You won't, Carl. There are some men who don't lose. I think you're one of them."

"What nonsense," he said and wiped his forehead.

The coffee heated and she poured two cups and sat down across from him. "I suppose you're wondering why father didn't want Nix or Owen to run for office."

"That had occurred to me," Heinz said.

"He never said, but I think it's because they dislike Yankees instead of understanding them," Cecilia said. She reached out and patted his hand. "Drink your coffee, Papa. You may have your second and third in the governor's mansion in Austin if your nerve holds out."

He looked at her, then said, "When I look back it seems like a long road."

"It's a longer road ahead," she said, raising her cup. "Here's to it."

Center Point Large Print
600 Brooks Road / PO Box 1
Thorndike ME 04986-0001 USA

(207) 568-3717

US & Canada:
1 800 929-9108
www.centerpointlargeprint.com